Sorry to love you

you

Again and Again

Doubty Noble

First Published in March 2022

ISBN: 978-93-5472-739-9

BLUEROSE PUBLISHERS
www.bluerosepublishers.com
info@bluerosepublishers.com
+91 8882 898 898

Cover Design:
Geetika Kandari

Typographic Design:
Tanya Raj Upadhyay

Distributed by: BlueRose, Amazon, Flipkart

Acknowledgement

DEDICATED TO ALL THOSE PEOPLE WHO WENT BEYOND THEIR LIMITS TO PROVE THEIR LOVE.

TO THE FRIENDS WHO NEVER LEFT IN THE BAD TIMES.

TO THE PEOPLE WHO BELIEVED IN BRINGING OTHER PEOPLE TO LIFE.

TO THE PEOPLE WHO LOST EVERYTHING WHILE CHASING THEIR LOVE

AND

TO ALL THOSE WHO HAVE LOST THEIR LOVE IN THE SEARCH FOR A PERFECT LIFE.

Preface

Most of the incidents recorded in this book actually occurred. This is the love story of every second couple in Punjab. Ranvir is a character drawn from real life, he combines the characteristics of two boys I knew from my school time.

Ibaadat, however, is a character who was very close to me during my school days. Passionate about her dreams, she wanted to explore the world and the person inside her. But she forgot what she left behind.

Sahil is the one who narrated this entire story to me seven years after leaving the school. And believe me, after reading this book, if you think that you have a person like Sahil in your life, consider yourself lucky.

Although my book is intended mainly for the purpose of entertainment for young minds, I have tried my level best to explain that, "If you love someone, put in the best efforts to keep them close. As it is said that not everyone is lucky enough to get their lost phone and lost love back."

- **DOUBTY NOBLE**

Prologue

She started walking away from him towards the airport entrance. He caught a glimpse of tears in her eyes as she was moving away from him. At that point in time, even if he wanted to stop her, he would not have been able to do so. Gradually, she merged into the crowd and went away from him and his life.

I could see tears in his eyes and a fake smile on his face. Being his childhood friend, I could easily tell the pain behind his smile. "Ranvir, what happened? That is enough, yaar. Let her go now; she is not coming back anyway," I told him, and gave him a pat on his back.

Ranvir should not have met her in the first place. It was neither her fault nor his; neither did she approach nor did he. It was all an accident that happened to them when they were in school.

People say that school is a sacred place where pupils go to learn and serve. But for them, it was to learn, love, and serve. Ranvir was just 16 years old when he fell in love with this girl. I don't know whether it was love or not from her side, but she was just 15 at that time.

What a time we survived, when a 90s lad could not afford a personal mobile phone while he was studying in high school. At that time, Facebook was trending, and WhatsApp was emerging as a new messaging app.

That 2G-era brought lightning-fast changes in their lives. It all started with a friend request. Before that, they were total strangers to each other. He didn't even know that she existed in school. But that Facebook friendship took a different turn in their lives.

Eager to add more friends to his virtual life, Ranvir sent a friend request to her. Her innocent-looking profile had him in the first go. He sent her a request, they became friends, then from friends to close friends, and then they got committed into a relationship.

But life had different plans for them. They broke up after three years because she wanted to pursue her studies abroad. On the other hand, Ranvir had nothing to do but look after his father's well-settled business. So as their paths took different roads, so did they.

I called him by his name many times, but he stood still for a few minutes, thinking about what had happened in his life. Dumb and foolish enough to ruin his life along with the rest of the people who were close to his heart. Deep inside, he knew that she was never coming back but still, following his heart, he decided to wait there till she departed.

At that time, I gave a thought to everything that took place in the last three months. It was just a waste of time and effort that Ranvir put in to make her feel the same way as he did. Then, again the same thought came to my mind that he should not have met her again.

The major crisis started when she came back after completing her studies and met Ranvir. There were mixed sentiments in Ranvir's mind. He was overly optimistic about meeting her after so many years, and the darker side was that she was there only for three months.

Chapter 1

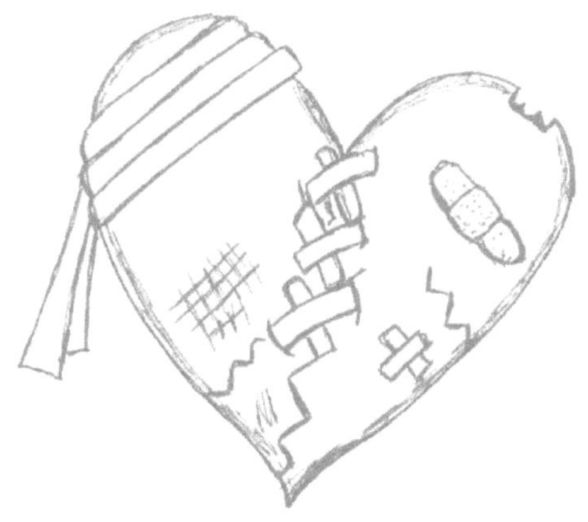

*P*unjab, a state known for its culture and festivals. The way in which we celebrate is class apart. From November to January, you are invited to attend one or the other function every weekend. Ranvir's family was well known in that area.

I remember that it was one of the Sundays in November when Ranvir's father wanted Ranvir and me to attend one wedding function to which the Sandhu family was invited. The invitation was by one of my uncle's friends.

"What will we do there? I don't even know anyone there," Ranvir questioned his father.

"Son, I would have never asked you to go, but today I have to go and attend another function in which my presence is of higher significance. So, you have no other option but to go there along with Sahil. Just hand over the shagun envelope to Mr. Bajwa and come back after having lunch," uncle replied.

We had planned to utilise the weekend in some other way, but we got stuck in a stupid function where we were like uninvited guests. We had an invitation, but it was for Ranvir's dad.

Suited and booted, we took our car and went to the Golden Galaxy resort. We went there at 1 PM and decided to come back at 4 PM. Ranvir recognised Bajwa uncle, so we went straightway to him and greeted him.

"Oh, hi Ranvir. How are you? I can't see your father around. Is he coming?" Bajwa uncle asked curiously.

"Uncle, he was willing to attend the wedding, but at the last moment, he got an important call regarding work. So he asked me to come and congratulate you and your family on this auspicious occasion." Ranvir bluffed at that moment. "Well, I wish he was here. Okay son, you enjoy it with your friend, and I insist that you both come to our house after this. We will have a great time together."

"Uncle, at least spare us some time for ourselves. Isn't it enough that we came here to attend this function?" I was thinking in my mind.

After that conversation, we went to a table laid down on the lawn, and sat there. Then, after a few minutes, the D.J. started the music at high volume. After that, girls, ladies, and aunties of all ages went to the dance floor and started dancing.

Even though most of them did not know how to dance, they were still enjoying it. Finally, Ranvir jumped up from his seat and asked me to go along with him. After getting bored, from there, we went to have something to eat and drink.

We got chicken for ourselves and went to the bar. After gulping a few shots, Ranvir was high. While waiting for the bartender to go for another round, Ranvir got up and started running away from me.

After drinking both of our shots, I went after him. By the time I caught up with him, I saw him standing next to a girl. I was standing at a distance from them, observing them silently, trying to figure out who the hell she was?

She was wearing a white and golden lehenga. Brown hair, face full of makeup. I could not recognise her as I was standing at a distance. As I went closer, I could not control my emotions.

"WTF........!! Ibaadat, what the hell are you doing here?"

Ibaadat, the girl who broke up with Ranvir six years ago, went away from him without even considering what he felt about her, didn't even try to find out how he was after she left, didn't talk to Ranvir in the past few years was standing in front of him smiling and talking to him as if nothing had happened.

When Ranvir went running toward her, he called out her name. Music was too loud for Ibaadat to hear Ranvir's voice. Ranvir was already high, and after seeing Ibaadat, he was on seventh Heaven.

Ranvir tapped on her back so that she could stop. Ibaadat was surprised to see him there. Their faces turned red in that spur of the moment. Ibaadat smiled and said, "Hi!" Both were confused in that situation- now what?

"What are you doing here? Weren't you supposed to be in Canada?" Ranvir yelled loudly to beat the D.J. volume.

"I came here to attend my cousin's wedding. Landed here a few days back. By the way, are you from the groom's side or bride's side?" Excited to take the conversation ahead, Ibaadat replied.

"Well, I am from the groom's side. Just came here on behalf of my father. Sahil came along with me as always. So, when are you planning to go back?"

"Going back? I am here for at least till the first week of February. But I think you are willing to send me back early, isn't it Ranvir?"

"No, I didn't mean that... I was just asking for how long are you here? You know I was never quite good with words," Ranvir replied, while thinking about something else.

"I wish I could keep you forever. If it would have been in my hands, I would have never let you go away. And you think that I want you to go early?"

They both were smiling at each other when I arrived at the point of action. I went close and gave a pat on Ranvir's shoulder.

"Let's go, man. We are getting late."

Ibaadat waved her hand towards me. "Hi Sahil, how are you? Nice to see you again."

"Oh hi! Wow, I was not expecting you here. Good to see you," I replied.

The last line was a bit of formality from my side. I knew it could never be good if Ibaadat was around, especially for Ranvir. But he never felt the same way.

"Do we have any work to complete right now?" Ranvir asked with a begging face.

"No, actually I have to do something important. That's why we need to go right now." And now it was my time to have fun with Ranvir.

But he replied, "Buddy, I am enjoying this party very much. Why don't you take the car and go? You can pick me up later."

I could not believe that. Ranvir never let anyone drive his car. It was like his second love. Things were reverting back to as they were six years ago. All I could see was the unconscious and irresistible love in Ranvir and Ibaadat's minds.

"Can't believe that you two are still together as you were six years ago. I have always dreamt of this kind of bond with my pals, but even now, I haven't got one as you have Sahil," Ibaadat said, while I was leaving.

"Well, I think I am lucky enough to have a friend like Sahil. He is always there for me as I am for him. A friend like him can make you feel like you are the best, and you can achieve whatever you want to."

Ranvir felt delighted while telling this to Ibaadat. She asked him whether he would be coming for the evening function or not. There was no reason to say no, so Ranvir, who initially did not want to come, was now ready to go for another round at Mr. Bajwa's house.

It is mistakenly said that love is blind. Love doesn't make sense, and the person who falls in love loses all of his senses. Ranvir was that stupid guy who lost everything just for his love. He even lost his loved one for love.

Ranvir used to say, "If you genuinely love someone, then you can't expect the same from that person. Love is unconditional and unforgettable, but for most people, these two things about love are unbelievable."

According to me, love is the craziest thing that can ever happen to a person. That day was one of the best days for Ranvir, when he was with Ibaadat. We went to Mr. Bajwa's house. Ibaadat was already there as if she was waiting for Ranvir to come.

They danced together as they used to do six years back. We came back extremely late that night, so I stayed at Ranvir's house. It seemed that Ranvir was in love again and again with the same girl.

Chapter 2

The following day, I was about to break his phone as it started ringing at 7 in the morning. Ranvir's mom came into the room with morning tea. She woke up Ranvir and inquired about Ibaadat. That was the name displayed on the phone screen with seven missed calls.

"Isn't she the same girl whom you were dating 6 years ago? Is she back here? How did you come in contact again?" So many questions in aunty's mind, but Ranvir was not prepared to answer any of them and that too when he was half asleep.

"Aunty Ji, they met at Bajwa's function. She is here for a few months, so they exchanged numbers just to stay in touch." I replied on behalf of Ranvir to calm his mom down.

"I better talk to her right now, or she will go crazy. Already 7 missed calls. I don't know what's going on in her mind right now." Ranvir texted her while taking a sip of his tea.

Ranvir- Hi.... sorry I could not pick up your calls. Good morning. How are you?

Ibaadat- Where were you since morning☹? I thought we could spend a day together, but I think you don't have time for me.

Ranvir- What? I am always there for you. Be it then, be it now, or be it tomorrow. Where do you want to go?

Ibaadat- Anywhere. Things have changed significantly in these 6 years, so I do not know much about this city.

Ranvir- Okay, I will pick you up by 10. Be ready and do not be late like you were always. ☺

Ibaadat sent a few pictures of different dresses asking Ranvir to decide what to wear.

Ranvir- I think you already know my and your favourite colour.

Ibaadat- Okay, done. Will be waiting... ☺.

Ranvir blushed, and he was glowing like anything while texting her. So, I guessed it right that they were going to meet. So just for fun, I started messing up with him.

"Buddy, I need you to go with me today. We have important work to do, and I can't do it alone." I knew that Ranvir never said no to work that concerned him.

But that day, Ranvir almost cried in front of me, and I could not control my laughter. Then, he gave a disappointing look. After that, I told him to go along with Ibaadat. And again, that smile came back.

He was so excited that he was ready by 9. The guy who used to take at least an hour to get ready was dressed up within minutes. Ranvir knew the reason behind me staring at him and replied in advance to my stare.

"That's the power of true love. Don't be surprised; I know what you are thinking right now. When it comes to Ibaadat, I can literally do anything for her, and I mean it."

Ranvir reached Ibaadat's house by 10. As he was moving towards the front gate, he started getting goosebumps as he remembered those good old days when he used to visit the same place almost every day.

He rang the doorbell and waited outside. As expected, Ibaadat was not ready on time. Instead, she insisted on Ranvir to come inside and meet her family. Ranvir was about to meet them after six years, and he was nervous about that.

He met everyone and went straight to the guest room as if he knew what was coming next. He was served with tea along with his favourite snacks by Ibaadat's mom.

"Have beta Ji. I still remember your favourite snacks that you used to have six years ago." Ibaadat's mom smiled.

Ranvir was sitting amongst Ibaadat's family talking about what had happened these six years while Ibaadat was still getting ready. Ranvir used to feel disgusted earlier while sitting like this, but he was enjoying that talk for the first time.

After taking an hour more, finally, Ibaadat came to the guest room. She was wearing Ranvir's favourite black suit. Although her makeup was noticeably light, she looked none less than a model.

Ranvir made a waaooo expression which was eminent. Thank you, she said without uttering a single word. Then, she smiled at his look, and he smiled back to say, let's go.

While they were communicating without speaking, Ibaadat's dad told them to go and come back safely.

"So where are we going today? What are your plans?" Ibaadat seemed so excited about everything that was happening around her. She felt like time had not passed at all in the last six years.

"Wow, you still ride this one. I love this car. It recalled all the memories from the past. Those long drives and everyday rides." Ibaadat gave him a quick hug and sat on the front seat even before Ranvir could react to that hug.

Ranvir, after requesting thousands of times, took his father's car. It was not the case that he had an average vehicle. But that was the same car which he used to drive earlier. So, he exchanged his brand-new Skoda for Corolla Altis for the next few months. The only reason behind all this was Ibaadat.

"So, where do you want to go? Shopping or breakfast?" Ranvir giggled as he knew that Ibaadat would be starving like hell.

"Why do you even ask when you know everything? Isn't it just to tease me?"

"Say no more. Just sit back and relax. You are about to experience some high-speed driving. So please, put on your seat belt." Ranvir winked and pushed the ignition button.

Chapter 3

anvir was very delighted after he came back. Then, without wasting any time, he straight away came to my house. The clock was ticking at 11:00 PM. I was watching Money Heist on Netflix while he came and knocked at my door.

"What's up, buddy? How was your first so-called date after a long time?" I opened the door with this question tossing straight on his face.

He could not stop blushing. It seemed like he was the happiest person living on this planet. "It was awesome, bro. We did all those things we used to do earlier. We had breakfast, then we went shopping, and it was pretty fun. She even hugged me. I believe that she is ready to come back into my life."

"Wait, what? She has just spent a day with you, and you were busy helping her buy new stuff. And it was barely a hug. How can you even think about it? Come on, man, grow up a little."

He got defensive when he said, "You don't know anything. We spent a whole day together, and that is enough for both of us to understand that we are ready to be back in each other's life." He folded his arms while I gave him an intense stare of judgement.

"Bro, I am telling you, the end is near." I smiled, went back to my bed, and continued watching Netflix. He sat on the chair kept next to the bed and started talking about her. "Sahil, do you know what we did the whole day?" He continued irritating me with his talk.

Ranvir didn't even realise that I was getting bored while listening to his nonsense. He kept on talking about Ibaadat, "Bro first we went to the mall of Amritsar, then we did shopping for three hours, and after that, we went to visit the golden temple. Finally, after having famous kulchas in Amritsar, we came back."

I kept on ignoring him, and finally, he said, "OKAY, leave it."

"That's like my boy. Leave it. In fact, leave her, bro. She is not worth wasting time for. Also, Tokyo died in the last episode." I kept a hand on his shoulder and acted like an older brother to him. He gave me a weird look like I had done something incredibly wrong.

At first, I thought that it was because of the spoiler. But then I realised that I had lost Ranvir again to the same girl who left him alone to cry six years ago. But for Ranvir, I was becoming a hindrance in his way to go back to Ibaadat. As for me, I was just trying to stop him from going back to that hell again.

The hell out of which it wasn't easy for him to come back, out of which he got nothing but pain, out of which he came back half dead. No, I could never see that happening again in front of my eyes.

While I was thinking about this, Ranvir's phone buzzed.

Ibaadat- Didn't sleep yet?

Ranvir- I was waiting for your text ☺.

"How the hell did you become good at lying?" I whispered.

Ibaadat- Oh..... so, you knew I was going to text you.

Ranvir- Oh, come on, this is not the first time I have spent a day with you.

Ibaadat- After so many days, I felt this good in my life; thank you so much. I couldn't even imagine my stay here without you.

I screamed in the middle of the night after seeing that text. "WTF is this? I don't know what this girl is up to. Do you think she is into you? I am sorry to say that, bro, but she is just using you to make her life comfortable and nothing else."

Ibaadat- You don't want to say anything?

Ranvir- I want to say a lot of things. Sahil is sitting next to me, and you know him right. He makes the conversation very difficult, especially when it is with you.

"You bitch," I interrupted again.

Ibaadat- Yeah, I know the things that have happened in the past have changed many things. I know he doesn't like me at all, but I am okay with that.

"And now this girl is heating things up in our friendship. I can't even imagine that you are still talking to her. Working for her as a personal assistant," I said in my frustration, and I believed that I was too harsh at him. But it was the need of the hour.

I couldn't believe what he said to me that day.

"I left her once when you said, I cannot do that again. So why don't you leave this up to me? I don't want your interference in this matter again, please."

"Can you hear what you are saying? You were getting off the track for that girl, and I was the one who brought you back. You know Ranvir, you are successful today just because Ibaadat went away, and I stopped you from chasing her," I said dumbfounded.

He didn't say anything and went outside. It was 1 AM, there was dead silence in the colony on the rooftop. Then, finally, I heard the clink of the bottle opener followed by the fizz of bubbles. I knew that the rooftop was Ranvir's favourite place when he wanted some time alone. A beer bottle was his companion.

We had placed a refrigerator full of beers and soft drinks on both roofs (Ranvir's place and my place). They were kind of minibars for us to enjoy. In fact, these roofs were our favourite places to sit and relax. We had made a pact while making these rooftop bars, "No matter what, even if we are facing the worst situation in life, we will just chill when we are here."

I got a bottle for myself and went near him. "Oye, RV........ let's go down and talk about this. I know that I was too harsh on you, but you know the reason behind it. So okay, from today onwards, I won't muddle with your matters."

"Cheers. Even I spoke more than I should have. You are also right but let me trust my faith once. Ibaadat came back, she met me at a function in which my presence was not even required, till now she doesn't have a boyfriend, and I am not seeing anyone either.. What do you think this is?"

Ranvir seemed very serious about her. But I was too afraid to lose my brother again. "Hold on, she doesn't have a boyfriend! Are you sure? Did she say this to you?" I asked in an astounding tone because I couldn't digest that a girl like Ibaadat did not have a boyfriend even after 6 years of break-up.

Ranvir took the last sip from his bottle and said, "Obviously, she is single. Otherwise, she would have told me if she were in a relationship. So now I want you to sleep tight and from tomorrow don't even think about her or, for that matter, us."

"Buddy, that was rude. But don't worry, whenever you need a shoulder to cry on, I will be here on this same rooftop. Just get your beer bottle, and we will talk." I said and went back to my room. Ranvir was sitting there for the next few minutes, and after that, he went back to his house.

I could not sleep that night, as I was worried about Ranvir. He was falling for the girl who once left him when he was more than ready to accept her as a life partner. To be honest, I didn't have a problem with their past, but even after she came back into his life, she was just using him.

I was worried just because he had a soft corner for Ibaadat. Ranvir hardly recovered from the break-up before, and again he was stepping into the same marshy trap of love.

Chapter 4

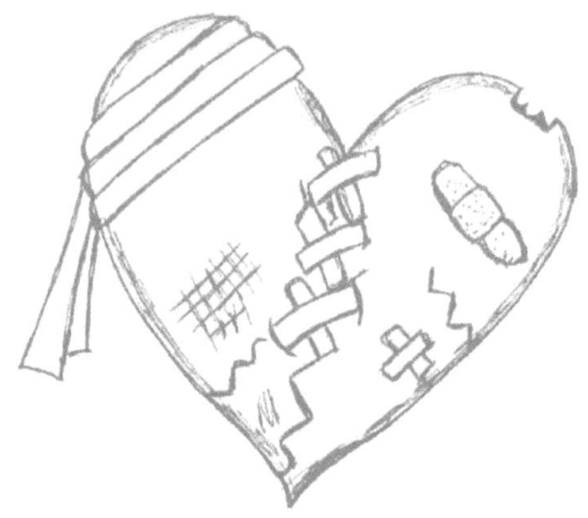

"The number you are calling is currently busy. Please try again later." I hate this tune, especially when I badly want to talk to someone. However, the following day this was the only voice I heard when I tried Ranvir's number.

I tried calling him many times, but his phone was on do not disturb mode. I was worried about him, so I went to his house to check up on him. Ranvir's mom was at the door when I rang the doorbell.

"Aunty, can you tell me where Ranvir is right now?" I inquired.

"I don't know beta, I thought he was with you. He just took the old car's keys and went outside. Is there a problem?" Ranvir's mom replied.

I just nodded my head and told her that everything was all right. But everything was going out of control. I was afraid that Ranvir had gone with Ibaadat again; otherwise, he would have taken his new car.

 Later, as I was heading toward the Nehru complex, what I saw on the road was utterly unbelievable to my eyes.

Ranvir was sitting alone in the car while Ibaadat was sitting in a shop with classmates from school. Ibaadat, Kavya, and Bhavya were best friends at that time. Ranvir used to tell Ibaadat that she should not have these girls in her company.

And that day, the same idiot was driving all three of them to get some stupid ice cream. I didn't know Ranvir would change for someone and the change would be so drastic. At first, I decided to go and talk to him, but then the words he said last night came to my mind.

I felt pity for him; the innocent little boy was just dancing around a girl in a misbelief that she would come back in his life. I just came back to my house and relaxed for a bit. I have a severe problem: I cannot see my close ones suffering before my eyes.

It was tough for me to stay home doing nothing while Ibaadat enjoyed being with her friends with Ranvir as her assistant. I don't know why, but I had developed an intense dislike for Ibaadat by then.

She was taking my best friend away from me. That was not the only issue; the main reason was that she was not staying in his life forever. And it was not happening for the first time with Ranvir.

Ranvir was very popular in school. In addition to that, he was good at every activity that took place in the school. But Ibaadat was a very innocent and introverted girl.

She created her Facebook profile on her mom's phone while she was in class 8th. Ranvir was looking forward to making new friends, so he sent friend requests to everybody in his suggestions list. Almost all of those friend requests were accepted.

By then, Ranvir was sure that all the girls from school would text him for sure. But, unfortunately, all his expectations were let down as no one texted him first. Then, finally, Ranvir got one message from Ibaadat, and that's how the blunder in his life began.

Ibaadat- Hi. How are you?

Ranvir- I am good. What about you?

Ibaadat- I am good too.

Ranvir- Do we know each other?

Ranvir was expecting that the girl he was talking to would have seen him in school. So, he was very eager to natter.

Many girls were crazy after him. There was no doubt in that. Sometimes even I was jealous of him because my girlfriend used to talk about him all the time. But Ranvir was not ready to be a part of any relationship. He was just a good friend of everyone.

He was focused on building his career ahead. He had a vision of becoming a business tycoon at that young age in which school kids talked about forgetting notebooks at home.

As expected, Ibaadat replied to Ranvir.

Ibaadat- I don't think you know me, but I know you very well.

Ranvir- Okay. So please if you can introduce yourself?

Ibaadat- Hey, I just know your name and class and that too because I have heard about you a lot. But I want you to introduce yourself as well.

Ranvir- All right, but ladies first ☺

Ranvir never gave his introduction first. He knew exactly what to talk about and how to talk.

Ibaadat- Ibaadat, I belong to Amritsar. 8ᵗʰ C.

A few years back in India, you couldn't expect a high school girl to put her picture on the profile; the same was the case with Ibaadat. But, there was no one to stop Ranvir from asking for her picture.

Ranvir- Can I see your photo? You know it is tough to talk without knowing the person in real.

Ibaadat- Photo?

Ranvir- Is there a problem?

Ibaadat- No, not at all. But don't show it to anyone else.

Ibaadat sent him a photo after some time. However, Ranvir couldn't recognise her even after seeing her photograph. Ibaadat was very disappointed after reading that Ranvir hadn't seen her in the school.

Ibaadat- Okay, we will meet in school then. I hope that you will be able to recognise me.

Ranvir- yeah, sure, that would be great.

Ibaadat- Okay, so tomorrow after school, we will meet in the auditorium.

Ranvir- Will be eagerly waiting.

Ranvir didn't sleep the whole night. He was wondering, who the hell was that girl? The girl who knew about him and on the other end of the table, Ranvir, was unaware that Ibaadat existed.

Starting from the morning assembly, he was very excited. That day he was filled with different types of vibes. He was looking for two eyes that were looking at him very carefully. He was more cautious about his actions in school than ever before. He told me everything once I asked him, "What's the matter with you?"

Period after period was passing, but for Ranvir, a minute felt like an hour. Then, finally, the clock ticked 01:30 PM. As soon as the school bell rang, Ranvir moved out of the classroom as if he had to catch the bus leaving in the next few seconds.

Ranvir straight away went to the auditorium; no one was there. He was very disappointed after seeing that. He checked the backstage, green room, and every possible place in the auditorium. Finally, after a few minutes of effort, he started walking out of the auditorium.

Disheartened and thwarted, he moved out of the auditorium. He was about to exit the school gate when he heard a voice. "Are you going out without seeing me?" Ibaadat was standing beside the outer wall of the school. Dressed in a cream shirt and green skirt, she was looking great even in the school uniform.

Ranvir turned around to her and was wondering how God could be so partial while creating her. He didn't speak anything at that moment and was continuously staring at her like a fool. Both of them were just smiling and didn't even bother to utter a single word during their first meeting.

The school bus was about to leave, I called out his name many times, but he didn't listen. Finally, Ibaadat asked him to go after seeing me shout out his name.

Ranvir came running towards the bus and entered while it was moving at a slow pace. Standing at the door of the bus, he waved goodbye to Ibaadat, and she smiled back.

Chapter 5

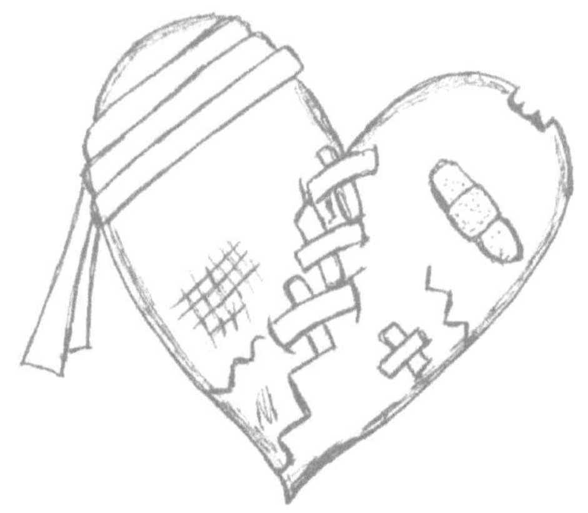

Ibaadat- Is this the way you treat her when you meet a girl for the very first time?

Ranvir- I don't know what happened to me? But let me tell you one thing,

You are gorgeous.

Ibaadat- HAHA. Thank you so much.

Ranvir- Hey! I am serious about that.

Ibaadat- Really?

Ranvir- Yes, of course!

Ibaadat- Thank you so much.

Ranvir couldn't control his emotions and was going crazy for her. She was all over his mind. Although they didn't talk much at that time, she was still in Ranvir's mind at every point in time. Whether in class or playground, be it at home or outside, Ranvir kept talking about her.

For a moment, I thought that Ibaadat would be going through the same situation, but I was wrong. It was only Ranvir who was acting otherwise. Ibaadat was very typical with these things going between her and Ranvir. Her normalcy was that she didn't think of Ranvir as more than a friend.

Every second year our school used to organise a Science Exhibition. Students were welcome to participate in it, and there was no restriction on the number of participants. Finally, the competition was announced open. This was a perfect opportunity for Ranvir to club with Ibaadat and do a project.

Even before I could advise him on this, he was all set with the plan. He had already talked to his I.T. teacher and was planning on doing a project on virtual reality. Fortunately, virtual reality was not ordinary in those days, and things were not available to everyone.

He wanted to talk about this to Ibaadat, but she didn't come to school that day.

Ranvir- hey, where were you today?

Ranvir texted her and was eagerly waiting for her reply. Finally, after waiting for two long hours, he got a text back from Ibaadat.

Ibaadat- Hi, I was busy today. Family functions, you know. What happened?

Ranvir- You know, the principal announced the Science Exhibition today.

Ibaadat- Oh! That's great. So, when is it?

Ranvir- Two months from now.

Ibaadat- Okay. So, what are we going to see from you this year?

Ranvir- This time, I will be working on virtual reality. I have talked to Khan sir about this. What are you planning to do?

Ibaadat- umm... I don't think I will be doing anything. I am not good at this.

Ranvir- What? How is this possible? Aren't you the topper of the class?

Ibaadat- Well, that doesn't mean that I will be good at innovations and stuff.

Ranvir- Okay.

Ibaadat- Yes.

Ranvir- By the way, you can join me if you want.

Ibaadat- Are you planning to lose this time?

Ranvir- No no no, you don't worry about that. I have planned it all.

Ibaadat- Okay, but what about your classmates and friends?

Ranvir- Naah, this time it's just Sahil and me.

Ibaadat- okay, but don't you think it will look odd? Like me working with you two boys and that too from a senior class.

Ranvir- Yes, it will, but it won't if you bring one of your friends along.

Ibaadat- Is it okay with you if I bring two?

Ranvir- Okay, no problem at all. By the way, who are they?

Ibaadat- Bhavya and Kavya.

Ranvir- Wait, wait, wait, are you sure? I don't think they know much about computers.

Ibaadat- Ranvir, I don't know much about this Virtual Reality thing either.

Ranvir- Okay, done. You can bring them along.

Although Ranvir was unwilling to work with Ibaadat's friends, he still agreed. And by that time, Ranvir had completely fallen for her but couldn't tell her.

The next day, Ranvir went to Ibaadat's class and took the teacher's permission to talk to her. She came out of the class and told Ranvir to call her friends too. So Ranvir went inside again and called both of them. It was just the first period in the school. They were allowed to go out of class because Ranvir called them. Ranvir had maintained an excellent reputation in the school and everyone saw the future head boy in him.

Then, they came to the staff room where I was waiting for them along with Khan sir. While they entered the staff room, Khan sir asked me just one thing, "Are you sure you want to work with these girls?" Khan sir already knew them as they were the least interested students in his class.

Khan sir asked the same question to all three of them. Before any of them could speak up and say something, Ranvir started explaining, "Believe me, Sir, it will be perfectly fine." He made a pleading face in front of him, and finally, Khan sir agreed on the team. He told us to use the I.T. Lab for the project.

So, we began with the project. While I was busy with it, Ranvir was busy with Ibaadat, and Bhavya and Kavya were only interested in moving out and bunking the class. For the first time in my life, I felt horrible while teaming up with Ranvir.

This continued for a while, and my frustration was increasing day by day. About forty-five days were left for the competition, and we couldn't figure out the details to be worked upon. Finally, on a perfect day, I could see Kavya and Bhavya in the I.T. Lab.

"Should I say welcome to our project?" I asked both of them as they entered the lab. But what I didn't notice was, Ranvir and Ibaadat were walking right beside them.

"What happened, Sahil? Why are you shouting at them?" Ibaadat inquired.

"Nothing, absolutely nothing, and that is the only problem here. I am the only one working on this project, and I am not getting any help from any one of you." I yelled at Ibaadat.

In the meantime, Ranvir tried to calm me down, but I was angry at him too. He was the one who got the idea of doing this project together, and he was the one who forgot the meaning of being together.

"Do you guys even understand what these forty-five days mean to us? Ranvir, you even promised

Sir that there will be no problem in doing this project and this goddamn virtual reality is a very difficult idea to work on."

I made sure that no one got offended there, but my words should give them an accurate picture of the situation in front of us. After that day, every member of the group was there to help with the project.

Finally, we were ready with the project, but it was not good enough to get the first prize. Ranvir tried his level best to do the task, but Ibaadat was a big distraction in his way.

Khan sir was very disappointed by our work; he blamed Ranvir as the project wasn't up to the mark. Finally, even after being one of the best, our work couldn't secure the runners-up trophy on the D-day.

It was a surprise for the entire school that the previous winner couldn't even secure top three positions. Ranvir didn't speak to anyone that day.

Chapter 6

The following day, I went to him to find out whether he was alright or not. I was astounded by what I saw that day; I saw a different Ranvir.

When I entered his room, he was doing some work on his computer. At first, I thought that he might be looking for the things that went wrong in our project, but when I went close to him, I saw that he was talking to Ibaadat on Facebook.

"Hi buddy, what's up?" I gave a pat on his shoulder while he was deeply involved in the conversation. He closed the Facebook window immediately.

"Nothing bro, I am just surfing on the internet." Ranvir stood up and covered the monitor facing me. I felt pity for him. He was saying that nothing had happened, but anyone could see that he was moving towards his own destruction.

"Bro, what's the matter with Ibaadat? Are you still planning to date her?"

"She is a nice girl. You know Sahil that I don't do this dating thing and all, but if I ever change my mind, then it would be for Ibaadat."

"Bro, she made you lose a competition in which you were the top contender. Maybe, I am wrong here, but still, my point holds more weightage than your probably one-sided love."

"I believe it's not one-sided, bro. She also likes me as much as I do; otherwise, she would have never participated in the science exhibition. We enjoy spending time with each other. Don't you think these are the signs of two-sided love?"

"Bro, you support her by going beyond limits, but just remember that she will leave you when she is at her best."

"Don't worry Sahil, anything can happen in this world but not this. One thing is for sure, she won't leave me when I need her."

I knew by then that I had lost my friend to a girl who he had met a few months ago. Instead of focusing on his career, Ranvir was busy with his love life. Ranvir thought that this thing would be confined to a few people. But this news spread like a forest fire, from one person to another, and in this way, even the school teachers were aware of Ranvir's relationship with Ibaadat.

But Ranvir didn't care at all. All he wanted was to spend time with Ibaadat. As the days passed, he became more confident that Ibaadat would say yes if he proposed to her.

One day he decided to confess to Ibaadat. I asked him about his plan, and he said, "Buddy, I don't have a plan. I will keep it very simple, just a red rose, and that's it. But I will do that in front of the whole school."

He went to the school on a very fine day and proposed to her with a beautiful red rose. He did that in public, and to my surprise, Ibaadat also said yes. So now, they were officially a couple in front of the whole world.

But I was happy for him; at least he was living his life to the fullest at that time. In fact, I was the one who organised their first party as a couple. They seemed very serious about this relationship. So, I said one thing to Ibaadat that day, "Don't make him feel special and leave him like he never mattered."

Ranvir was so excited that he even told his mom about this. Ibaadat did the same with her mom. It was hard for me to believe that at the age of 14, they told their parents that they wanted to marry each other.

But this wasn't the end of the story. This story took a different turn when Ranvir completed his 10th and went to a different school. They both were separated by distance.

Earlier, they spent the whole day together, but Ranvir couldn't see her regularly after changing schools. After that, however, Ranvir visited Ibaadat's home frequently. They put in all their efforts to continue the relationship for one year, but some major crisis started when Ibaadat shifted to a girl's hostel to pursue higher studies.

They were in different cities, and it was challenging to talk every day. Ibaadat was not allowed to keep a phone there. So, it was kind of a cut-off for two years. They met only when Ibaadat came back from the hostel.

But I believe that this period was the best time for Ranvir to focus on his career. So, after completing his 12th we both got admission in one of India's top universities for our graduation.

It was a very proud moment for our families, but one person didn't seem happy after hearing this news. Everyone believed that Ranvir would do something great in life. But some people didn't think that way, and Ibaadat was on the top of the list.

45

Chapter 7

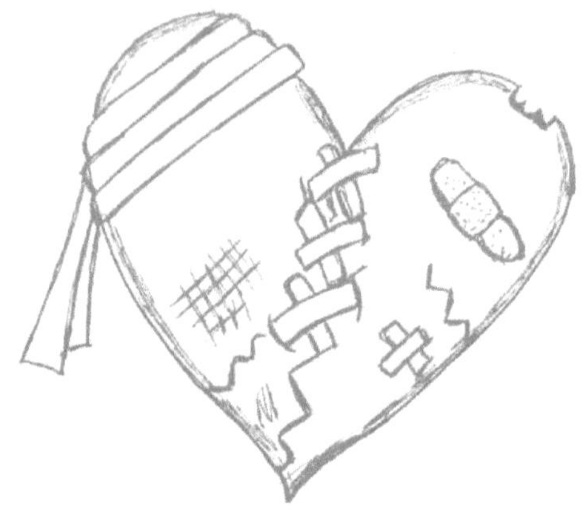

After finishing her 11th grade exams, Ibaadat came back home. Ranvir went straight to her house when he got that news. Ranvir was very excited to meet her and tell her about his admission. But, she was more shocked than surprised.

"I hope your exams went well. You were worried during that time." Ranvir said to start the conversation.

"Yes, they were good. Mom told me that you wanted to say something. What is it?"

"You know Sahil and I, we got selected in Symbiosis university for our further studies. Your boyfriend will be running his own chain of business very soon."

"Good Ranvir, I am very happy for you. But you know what, I have decided to go to Canada after 12th for higher studies."

"What? Are you sure you want to go away? But what about us then?"

"I don't know Ranvir, but one thing is for sure that I am going to Canada' and most probably, I will be applying for citizenship too. But you know there is one solution to this problem."

Ranvir got an idea of what was coming next, but he still wanted to hear from Ibaadat. Ibaadat told Ranvir to come to Canada instead of joining Symbiosis so that at least they could be together.

"I am afraid that this has to end. Because I want to live here, settle here along with my friends and family. I don't want to be a lone survivor there." Ranvir tried to explain.

Ibaadat was very disappointed after hearing this from Ranvir, but she preferred to stay quiet instead of replying. Although Ranvir tried to lighten things up, it turned out differently.

"I love you, and I want you to know it."

"Love me how, Ranvir?"

"Why does this have to come down like this?" Ranvir questioned in frustration.

"Love me how?" Ibaadat said this, and Ranvir stayed quiet for a while

"That's what I thought. So, you either can't answer, or you won't answer it, which is bullshit because obviously, you don't just look at me that way. You are capable of looking at me that way, but you don't let yourself lose anything because you are afraid of risking everything."

"Look Ibaadat, the only reason that I don't want to go is that we have everything."

"No Ranvir, you have everything. You got selected in Symbiosis. But what about me? Where will I find space in your dreams of becoming a successful person in life."

"So, you want everything, Huh!"

"I don't know Ranvir. All I know right now is that I don't want your pity."

Ranvir didn't say anything after that, and he came straight to my house. He told me everything that happened at Ibaadat's place. He was crying out loud, and it was very difficult for me to see him in this condition.

I tried to make him stop crying, but he said, "Bro, please stop her; otherwise, she will ruin everything." So, I asked him if I would talk to Ibaadat, but he said it was pointless.

"Then we have to find some other solution. But first of all, you stop crying. You don't worry till the time your brother is alive." I told him by patting his shoulder.

A few days passed like this; I was worried about Ranvir. Then I thought that I should talk to

Ibaadat about this. I didn't tell Ranvir about this. Instead, I texted Ibaadat to meet her, and to my luck, she agreed instantly.

We were sitting at a cafe when we talked about this. It is rightly said that a lot can happen over coffee, and so it did that day.

"I heard that you had a fight with Ranvir. Are you sure that you want to go to Canada?" I asked her this without wasting any time.

"Look Sahil, everyone has plans for the future, and the same is true for me. Talking about Ranvir, I don't find myself in his future. That's it. Sometimes you just need to be practical in life while keeping your feelings aside."

For an instant, I just felt that she was right. But Ranvir wasn't wrong either. The only thing that pinched me was when Ibaadat asked Ranvir to go to Canada. So, I asked her about that.

"Sahil, I also want to live a life with him but why should I be the one to give up on my dreams? Don't you feel that this is an injustice to me?"

"I agree entirely with you Ibaadat, but you can't make him sacrifice his dreams for you. So, if it's not working, just don't ask him to push it further. It will ruin his life."

"If you think that Ranvir and I should stay together, then please make him understand that this is the only solution." Ibaadat was demanding too much. This made me furious and what I said next, changed the tone of our conversation

"You want him to sacrifice himself for you, and you, you are not worth it. Because you don't love him, you were just attracted to him."

"You are upset, and so is your friend." She said aloud.

"Oh, thank you, at least you think that."

She just went away after hearing this. How could she leave the conversation in between like this? I was furious at her. So, I asked Ranvir to meet me at my place.

Ranvir was not in a good mood to talk but it was essential for him to know what Ibaadat thought about him. I wanted him to be firmly standing on his decision. So, I told him that Ibaadat didn't care whether you would be good or not without her. All she wanted was to follow her dreams.

I didn't explain him in detail and just told him not to talk to Ibaadat anymore. He trusted me so much that he didn't even ask me why. But he said that he would like to speak with her on the day she would be leaving.

Finally, one day when Ibaadat left India, Ranvir celebrated the first failure of his life in style. He organised a party for Ibaadat to which limited people were invited. In his farewell speech, he mentioned their good times together and wished her luck for the future.

"You know, one day, I hope we meet again. And I wish that we get a chance to finish our story because it wasn't meant to end like this. So, I am going to focus on myself, and I hope that you focus on yourself too, and until we meet again, I wish nothing but the best for you."

I could see tears in his eyes, and this was the first time I saw him drinking. So, I just took my glass and stood next to him. Ranvir was looking at

Ibaadat while she was having fun with her friends, and he said, "People are afraid of thorns, but you know what? I have been bruised by roses."

After that day, Ranvir never saw Ibaadat, but he was always talking about her. She went to Canada the next day and never looked back. So, I personally thought that this was the end of everything. But as it is said, every ending is a new beginning.

Ranvir tried to contact her, but she didn't want to take anything from the past. So, she changed everything, her number, her Facebook ID, Instagram, and even herself. They were out of touch until she came back and accidentally met Ranvir.

Chapter 8

$\mathcal{I}$n those 6 years, Ranvir suffered from depression. As a result, he became very insolent, arrogant, and ignorant. He didn't talk much and was utterly goal-oriented. Moreover, he had developed a hatred for the people who went to foreign countries to settle in life.

He was very ambitious about doing something great here to set an example for all those who left their country just for the sake of settling in life. I saw remarkable progress in his marks as he advanced in his studies.

After completing his graduation, Ranvir offered me to work with him to establish our own chain of restaurants. So, I joined him up, and we started working on that.

He was full of great ideas, which made our work easier. Within two years, we opened two restaurants. Ranvir named the restaurants after Casanova because he believed that he should be one. He presented himself as a stud in front of the world but, deep inside, he knew that he was just a poor little boy striving for someone's love who was never coming back for him. There were only two people who knew about this; just Ranvir and me.

Our business was growing at a fast rate. It was a very proud moment for us when Ranvir's dad was called by his name at a social gathering. That was the day when uncle said, "Ranvir, you have made me proud today. You are a perfect example of a child that a father could ever ask for."

While driving back, Ranvir suddenly stopped the car and started crying. I was surprised by his behaviour; he had never done that before. So, I asked him what happened and what he replied was shocking.

"My parents think I am fine, my friends think I am fine, some days even I believe I am fine. But I am not; I am not fine at all. And I don't know how much longer I can pretend."

I knew the reason behind this, but I was helpless at that time. With time, the intensity of his crying increased, and Ranvir literally started praying to God for Ibaadat to come back in his life.

I believe that when we pray, we should say exactly what we want. But Ranvir asked half of his desires wholeheartedly. Finally, his prayers were answered, and she was back in his life.

Almost one entire month passed away like this. Ranvir was roaming around Ibaadat like her personal assistant. Then, Ibaadat planned a trip to Rajasthan with her friends, and she wanted someone to drive her there.

So, she asked Ranvir to go along. Ranvir asked if I could accompany them too. Ibaadat resisted at first, but then she agreed. When Ranvir brought this trip to my notice, I was mad at him.

I tried to explain to him again and again that Ibaadat was just using him for her own good, and she wasn't doing it for love. Ranvir requested me to give him at least one last chance to prove himself.

So, we planned a 5 days trip to Rajasthan, starting from Jaipur, the city of love. We reached there in the evening and were tired as hell. So, we called it a day and went to the hotel.

For the next two days, we visited all the famous places in Jaipur. Of course, the most memorable part of Jaipur was the hot air balloon ride. But, it was memorable in a different way for all of us. Only two people were allowed to ride at one time. Bhavya and Kavya wasted no time to pair up.

I was looking at Ranvir while he looked at Ibaadat. I regret it still, but I asked Ranvir to pair up with Ibaadat. But then, I was forced to pair up with some other tourist.

It was one hour of a ride, and in that one hour, a lot happened between Ibaadat and Ranvir. When they reached the maximum height, Ibaadat said, "Wow...No wonder Jaipur is called the city of love."

Ranvir, excited to talk about love, said, "Yes, it is said people find their soulmate here. But, I don't want to find anyone when you are there."

Ibaadat was dumbfounded after hearing that, but she didn't say anything. Instead, she asked him to enjoy the ride. Ranvir asked her if she wanted to say anything to him.

Ibaadat replied, "Ranvir, it has been six years. But, I find you standing at the same place as you were. You know, when I moved to Canada, a lot happened over there."

"I know Ibaadat, I have changed a lot too, but I am still the same for you," Ranvir spoke before Ibaadat could finish.

Ibaadat said that she just wanted him to be his good friend. When she asked Ranvir why he loved her even after they broke up, he replied, "It's not because you left me. It's because through this entire time I have still been waiting for you. When you left me, you never even looked back. But I have been waiting."

Ibaadat wanted to say something, but she was stunned after hearing what Ranvir said. On the other balloon, Bhavya and Kavya were enjoying themselves, and I was just staring at Ranvir and Ibadat until we landed.

We went to Khimsar for desert camping. Two days with no internet. But it worked pretty well for Ranvir and Ibadat. However, I was sick and tired of listening to Bhavya and Kavya's chin-wags.

The best thing about the camp was the campfire. People were free to dance, sing or express themselves. We danced away that night till 2 AM in the morning.

Everyone in the camp went off to sleep. The bonfire was still on, and there were five of us sitting beside it. One by one, we also started moving towards our tents. However, Ranvir and Ibaadat were still sitting there.

There was a remarkable fall in temperature as the bonfire started extinguishing. Ranvir and Ibaadat came closer to each other, feeling each other's bodies.

Ibaadat could hear Ranvir's heartbeat as she sat ahead of Ranvir. Ibaadat said, "I think we must go inside too." Ranvir resisted and said just ten minutes more. Ranvir took her in his arms.

There was one more person awake at the time. The DJ played the song "Perfect" by Ed Sheeran, and Ibaadat asked Ranvir for a dance. So they got up, had romantic eye contact and came closer to each other.

Ranvir put his arm around Ibaadat's waist and pulled her closer. Then, Ranvir started singing along with the music, "We were just kids when we fell in love."

They were sinking into each other's eyes. Ibaadat held Ranvir's face with both her hands and pulled him closer for a kiss. They kissed till the song ended.

Ibaadat said she wanted to tell him something, but Ranvir didn't allow her to say anything. Ranvir said, "I love you, Ibaadat. Let's get back together as we were," and again started kissing her.

Ibaadat tried to get herself away, but Ranvir didn't allow her to do so. She was stressed out, and finally, she pushed Ranvir away and went to her tent.

Ranvir was astonished after seeing that behaviour from Ibaadat. But he couldn't do anything about that. Even before he could recover from the shock and react, Ibaadat was in her tent.

Chapter 9

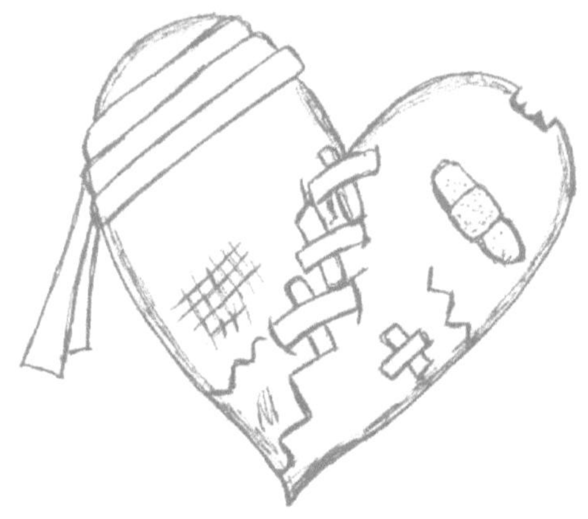

That Trip to Rajasthan proved to be a complete blunder in Ranvir's life. Ranvir and Ibaadat were together for four days; they enjoyed their life to the fullest.

It was the last day of our stay at Udhampur. Ranvir and Ibaadat were entirely over each other's minds. They were lost in their world when a person from a whole new universe made a surprise entry.

It was like a wild card entry that Ranvir was not expecting at all and that too in Rajasthan. Harry landed at the Delhi terminal and decided to join Ibaadat for her journey back home. Instead of going back home first, he booked a cab to Jaipur.

We were sitting in a restaurant enjoying our food. Then, all of a sudden, there was complete silence in the restaurant. It was like the silence before the storm, and then a sudden storm in the form of a tall, muscular, handsome guy appeared at the main door.

He was approaching our table, and I could see the spoon in Ibaadat's hand go still. Ibaadat was surprised to see him in Jaipur. Ibaadat stood up as he came near her and greeted him differently. "Harry, what are you doing here? You didn't tell me that you were coming to India. How come you landed up here?"

"Well, I thought I should give you a surprise. Your mom told me that you were in Udhampur today along with your friends. So, I came directly to see you. By the way, aren't you going to introduce me to them?" Harry said curiously.

"Okay, so guys, this is Harry, a family friend, and Harry, this is Kavya, Bhavya, Sahil, and Ranvir," Ibaadat replied anxiously.

"Oh! So here he is, Ranvir; she used to talk about you a lot while we were there in Canada. By the way, I would like to introduce myself as well, I am Ibaadat's to-be fiancé."

"You are what?" I had coke which spit out of my mouth after hearing that from Harry. Ibaadat never told Ranvir about Harry since the day she came back. She should have told him this on the first day, but she hid this truth from everybody.

"Oh! Weren't you all aware of this fact? I see..... Can we have a conversation in private?" Harry compelled Ibaadat.

"Talk in private? Yeah sure. Okay, guys, I am done with my meal. Anyone left can shift to the other table. Let them talk in private." Ranvir said in an astonishing and worried tone. I could feel him at that time.

"Ranvir, hold on for a second; you don't need to do all that," Ibaadat said and asked Harry to go along with her. Ranvir was acting as if no one would notice his abnormal behaviour. But he completely lost his mind that day.

"Kavya, were you aware of this?" I asked Kavya while Ranvir was sitting numb there on the table.

"Yes, of course, we were aware, and we thought that Ibaadat must have told Ranvir about this," Kavya replied to save herself. And that's it, end of Rajasthan tour. But, unfortunately, the whole fun, the entire trip was spoiled by just one moment.

We were returning from the trip. Ibaadat didn't come back with us. She preferred to stay back with Harry and spend some time. Meanwhile, I was thinking of killing her. It was a big blunder that Ibaadat created again. Ranvir was so confident that Ibaadat would be single as he was, but no. The most important thing was that she lied to him.

"Why the hell during this whole vacation did she lie to you? Even if she had told the truth, you would have still done the same things for her as you were doing till today." I shouted these words loud and clear so that everyone sitting in the car could hear.

Ranvir was sitting on the co-driver's seat from where he replied in an extremely low tone, "Maybe she was afraid that I would get hurt after hearing that?"

And that made the girls sitting behind laugh, which made me feel pity at Ranvir. "Oh my God! Are you able to hear what you are saying right now?" Ranvir put on his sunglasses so that he could hide his tears.

After a long day of travel, we reached Amritsar the following day. We dropped the girls home, and then I drove the car to Ranvir's house. Ranvir got out of the car and went to his room. He didn't talk to anyone in the house and locked himself in.

I told Ranvir's mother that he got too tired during the journey, so he wanted to take some rest. "I will come and see you in the evening," I said this and took leave from aunty. I was also tired as I drove the entire route back home. So, I went home and slept off.

In the afternoon, mom brought lunch for me. Then, I woke up and called on Ranvir's number, but it played the same tune that I hate so much. "The number you are trying to reach is currently busy." So, I called upon his mom's phone to check on him.

Ranvir's mom seemed a little worried about him as he was not responding to any of the knocks on his door. I went to his house and called out his name loud at his door. After doing that for at least half an hour, I got frustrated and shouted at him.

"Oh, come on! Ranvir, just tell me what is your fault, your mother's fault, or my fault in all of this. She was always like this, but you never noticed. She had always used you and left you. And you, my brother, was always blinded by love."

Ranvir's mother heard that and came running to me to ask if Ibaadat had said something. "No, aunty, she didn't say anything. That's where the problem lies. She didn't tell Ranvir anything about Harry. And you might be pleased to know that she is getting engaged by the end of January."

Ranvir heard that as I was intentionally loud so that at least he could come outside. "I just want some peace of mind. Can you please stay quiet?"

"Okay, so now you want us to stay quiet. No problem, I am going. Just give me a call if you want to talk about this." I said this and went away from him. I went to the wine shop and got three bottles of Jameson.

I returned to Ranvir's house and told aunty to tell Ranvir that I am sitting on the roof whenever he comes out of his room. So, I started waiting for him from 7 o'clock. I don't know if it was natural, but the time was passing very slowly. Every second felt like an hour.

8 PM, 9 PM, 10 PM, and finally, I saw him coming at 11 PM. He was carrying beer bottles in his hands. "Welcome brother, I have been waiting for you since 7 PM." Then, with a lowkey smile on his face, he came near me, and we sat on the edge of the roof facing the road.

There was deadly silence floating in the air around us. For a few minutes, we just kept quiet, looking at the road and people passing by. I could recollect the same scene from the past, six years back. After some time, I giggled a bit to which he said, 'What? Why are you laughing?' I could read agony on his face.

"Oh, come on, dude, there are almost 8 billion people in this world. You cannot spend your whole life crying over a girl who broke your heart twice. It is high time to face reality. Let's go out and find someone worthy of the love that you have shown to that girl." I filled two glasses with Jameson, and it was unbelievable that he said cheers to it.

"Well, maybe it is time you forget about her?" I spoke.

He didn't say anything, and the day ended with one bottle down. But, to be honest, I was worried about him, so I didn't leave him alone at any point in time.

Chapter 10

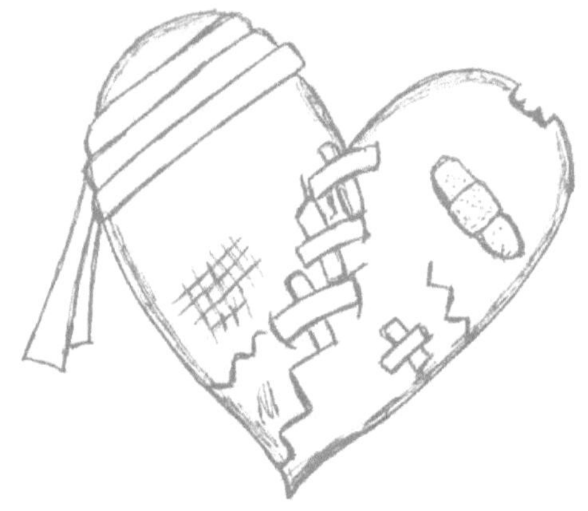

$\mathcal{I}$ wanted Ranvir to move on with his life. And by then, I was thinking about what should be done so that he doesn't think about Ibaadat. So, I decided to distract him by taking him to parties and clubs.

One fine night we were sitting in a bar. We had vodka shots sitting on the bar stools, and I saw two girls entering the bar. One of them was looking so beautiful that I was no longer sober. However, I could not understand whether it was vodka or her eyes that were hitting me hard.

To our luck, they both came and sat on the stools right next to us. So, I thought that this was the right situation Ranvir should be put into. I told Ranvir, "Hey buddy, I am going to talk to one of those girls. Do you want to come along?"

"Naah, I am good. All the best." Ranvir replied with a wink raising his glass. As I approached with an offer to drink, the girls started laughing, making fun of me. Disheartened and dejected, I came back and sat on the barstool beside Ranvir.

Ranvir patted me on my shoulder and said that it was alright. I agree that a person must learn to face failure while approaching a girl, but that was too much to handle.

I ordered four large while Ranvir was still on his second drink. He asked me to go slow. After having those inside me, I was no longer sober. Ranvir was in his senses and was trying to keep a hold of me.

After some time, I saw one of those girls turning her face towards me, waving her hand as if she was calling me. For an instance, I thought it was because of alcohol, but I went to her when Ranvir assured me that she was actually calling.

I went to her, and we started talking. Then, finally, I got a chance for an introduction. I got to know her name and profession. Ravneet was a dentist by profession. But what she said after the introduction was again disappointing.

"Hey, can you help in setting up my friend with yours?" She asked. She was not interested in me, but her friend was in Ranvir, which was why I was jealous of him. But that was the sole reason for coming to the bar that day.

"Okay, I will, but you have to tell her to follow exactly what I say." So, we had a little conversation, and I came back to Ranvir. He asked whether it was a yes or no? I said that she just wanted a complimentary drink and nothing else.

After some time, I told Ranvir that I was going to the washroom and would come back in a few minutes. Meanwhile, Girls were going for the third round of magic moments. So then, as planned, I gave a sign to Ravneet to move aside and texted Ranvir a few lines that worked like magic.

Buddy, I am so sorry, but I got an emergency call from one of my friends, so I went out straight from the club and reached his place. It will take about an hour, and I will be back. So just chill, and by the way, the girl sitting next to you is worth trying for.

We both went to one corner of the bar and allowed Ranvir to take his time to initiate the talk. Ranvir was mad at me, and the first thought that came to his mind was why he would ever want to do what I told him. So, he was just sitting there quietly, cursing me for leaving him like that. He was reading my message again and again.

Ranvir's face turned from angry to happy while reading between the lines. Then, slowly, he turned his face towards that girl. At least half of the bar was staring at her, and she was looking at Ranvir. Then, all of a sudden, a guy came near her and offered her a drink. Ranvir saw her transition from icy cool to hot lava in a few seconds.

She was too harsh on that guy, and I wondered what she would have done to Ranvir if he had approached her first. Ranvir was low on confidence in those days, so he stepped back and sat quietly on his bar stool.

He turned his face towards her, there was eye contact, and Ranvir turned his face away out of embarrassment. The second time when he turned his face towards her, they both smiled. Again, Ranvir turned his face away after a few seconds.

'What are you doing, dude?' Ranvir was thinking in his mind. And finally, after seeing Ranvir completely failing to approach, the girl came near him. "Hi, how are you?" she smiled and raised her glass.

"Haaaaaiiiiiiii..." Ranvir's voice fumbled while he raised his glass. He was pretty under-confident, maybe because of the girl's attitude. "Noor." She said her name and inquired about Ranvir.

"It seems like either you are too strong or too broken that you have come to a bar alone. So, which one goes true for you?" Noor smiled and finished her drink.

"My friend was there with me, but he managed to escape leaving me here with you. By the way, both of these are true for me." Ranvir winked and smiled.

"Do you want another one?" Ranvir took a shot of vodka and offered it to her. She took that and bottoms up in the next few seconds. Ranvir was astonished and offered her another one. This continued for the next 15 minutes, after which both of them were high.

"So, what about you? Single or committed?" Ranvir asked after gathering some courage. "Why do you think I am sitting here with you? Of course, I am single." Noor replied.

Finally, they got themselves a meaning for the conversation. This continued for the next two hours, and none of them was in senses. I reached out to Ranvir and said hello to Noor. We went home at 3 AM. Ranvir could not recall anything from their first meeting.

The following day Ranvir woke up at 11 AM, and the first thing he said was, "WTF, how did she get my number?" Meanwhile I was wondering, why is he so lucky? He exchanged his number with the most beautiful girl in the bar on the very first meeting, which he can't even remember.

Noor- Hi there. Noor this side.

Ranvir- Hi. How are you?

Noor- I am good. I just texted you to tell you that you are still a kid who cries for everything but doesn't do anything about it.

I was reading the messages too, "Bro, did you tell her your entire story last night? Unbelievable!"

"No, brother, I don't even remember talking to her. When you left, I just said Hi to her, and then after a few minutes, you came back. That's it." he replied, worrying about what happened last night.

"Few minutes! Bro, we were watching you talking to her for three hours straight. You know how boring it was to see you two talking..." Before I could complete myself, Ranvir interfered.

"What? You were watching me? Why did you do that?"

"Because I wanted you to get rid of your ex-girlfriend, you dumbo. Ravneet came to me to set you up with her friend," I replied furiously. He was still confused about whether he should continue talking to her or not. Finally, I forced him to respond.

Ranvir- I am sorry, I don't remember anything about last night.

Noor- Ha-ha, don't worry, I won't tell anyone about this.

Ranvir- Well, thank you so much, and please let me know if we can meet again over a cup of coffee.

Noor- Sure. Wednesday, 5 PM, Starbucks?

Ranvir- Perfect. See you then.

Okay, so now Ranvir was set for a date with Noor, and I had mixed feelings of happiness and jealousy for him. I told him to ask for a double date, but he said no to that without asking Noor. But he assured me that he would talk about Ravneet and me to Noor. So, I kept my feelings to the side and supported him so that he could completely forget Ibaadat, who had gone far away from his life.

After a very long time, I saw him getting excited about something. Otherwise, he was like, "SO WHAT?" Even for the happiest moments, he had developed this attitude. And this was turning him into a person that he never wished to be.

But that day, I saw my friend coming back to life. All thanks to Noor that Ranvir was turning into a happy person again. He bought new clothes just to have a cup of coffee with Noor. That was the first time when I felt that Ranvir could finally forget Ibaadat.

Chapter 11

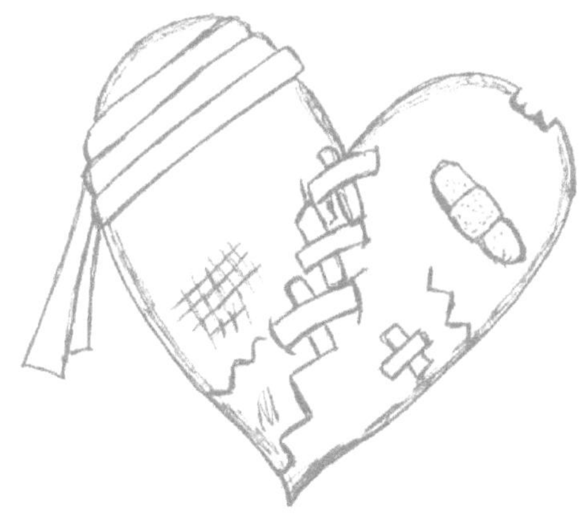

The clock was ticking at 4:30 PM; I was driving back to Ranvir's house so that he could take my car to meet Noor. Ranvir believed he would ruin everything if he took his car.

Ranvir was calling me frequently because he was getting late for his first actual meeting with Noor;

as such, there was just a blurred memory in his mind of the first one.

"Where were you, Sahil? I have been waiting for you since 3 PM." Ranvir was very angry at that time. I asked him to relax a little bit. He had at least a fifteen minute buffer to reach Starbucks.

This was for the first time that he was late for a date. He reached there five minutes late and was very embarrassed after seeing Noor sitting at one of the tables waiting for him.

Maybe she was a soothsayer, or it was just a coincidence that her outfit was exactly of Ranvir's choice. Noor wore a black dress, straightened hair, and her shining earrings gave an extra grace to her beauty.

Ranvir came close to her and apologised at the first instance for being late. After that, he just took his seat and waited for Noor to start the conversation. Noor's beauty was making him under confident while sitting with her.

"You know, for the first time in my life, I have waited for someone and that too for 10 minutes," Noor sounded upset.

"10 minutes? But I reached here at 5:05. How does that make 10 minutes?" Ranvir was thinking in the meanwhile Noor replied that she had been sitting there since 4:55. Just because she felt that Ranvir would be there by that time.

Then there was complete silence as if the time had stopped for them. Ranvir was just looking at her face and thanking God for that moment in the bar where he met Noor. But he wasn't aware that there was a lot to come. He saw Ibaadat entering the place with Harry.

"Hello.....! Will you speak something, or is it going to be a monologue again?" Noor asserted, but Ranvir didn't respond. Noor was surprised after seeing his behaviour.

Noor waved her hand in front of Ranvir's eyes while he fixed his eyes on Ibaadat. Seeing that Ranvir came back to where he was sitting. He apologised to Noor and said that he was driven into someone's thoughts.

"Okay, so Mr. Ranvir, tell me something about yourself?" Where are you from, and what do you exactly do for a living?" Noor asked.

"Let me help you out with this. I don't like answering questions." Ranvir replied arrogantly, which was surprising for Noor.

Noor was a perfect girl who was admired by all. This type of behaviour was new for her. But, instead of getting angry at Ranvir, she tried to find out the reason behind his arrogance.

Ranvir continued looking at Ibaadat, and after some time, Noor noticed that. So, she asked, "Ranvir, is she the same girl you were crying after last time?"

"Another question, Noor. Did you order the coffee yet?" Ranvir replied.

"I don't like ordering things. You should do that." Noor replied, irritated by Ranvir's tone.

"I hate her, but I love her, I miss her, but I am better off without her. I want her, but out of my life." Disheartened and discouraged, Ranvir said this from his mouth, but he was loud enough to be audible to Noor.

"Oh! So, I was right about that girl. But, you know what, some people only come into your life to show you what love is not."

"Hey, just because it didn't last forever doesn't mean it wasn't real. Even if it wasn't real from Ibaadat's side, I loved her from the bottom of my heart." Ranvir tried to defend his lost love.

Ranvir was bothered by Ibaadat's presence, aware that she was ruining his coffee date. So, he tried to save his date and ordered coffee. On the other side, Noor was amused by Ranvir's behaviour.

Meanwhile, having coffee, Noor teased Ranvir by saying that she could help if he wanted to meet Ibaadat at that time. Ranvir asked Noor to stay quiet for some time, but she was not ready to do that.

"Seeing her with someone even when you are on a date hurts you this much. I don't know how to say this, but Ibaadat has ruined your life to such an extent that now you don't know how to handle it." Noor said and started smiling.

"What if this pain was never meant to part from me?"

"Don't worry, Ranvir. Sometimes scars need a deeper cut in order to heal. And, I believe that these scars cannot be left on their own to heal at this time."

Noor was determined that she could change Ranvir and bring him back to life. However, she wasn't aware that the dead can not be raised to life again. Ranvir explained very clearly to Noor that he wasn't looking for any kind of relationship at that point in time.

Ranvir took a sip of coffee and said, "Staying alone is like a drug, and right now, I am completely addicted to it from tip to toe. But, believe me, once you are addicted to it, any drug will not suffice you."

"Except for love," Noor replied.

By that time, Ranvir saw Ibaadat and Harry moving out. Ibaadat didn't even notice that Ranvir was sitting there. Ranvir requested Noor to move out at that time. And finally, Ranvir and Ibaadat made eye contact in the parking area, which was a coincidence for Ibaadat but intentional from Ranvir's side.

Ibaadat told Harry, and within a few seconds, all four were standing next to each other. After a formal greeting, Ibaadat asked Ranvir about the girl standing next to him.

Noor, without any hesitation, replied to Ibaadat's question, "Oh, you Don't know. So Ranvir didn't tell you, huh? We have been dating each other for three years."

This was shocking for everyone standing there. However, Ranvir stood numb and didn't say anything. He just made an embarrassed face in front of Ibaadat and waited for both of them to leave.

Ibaadat seemed to be in shock after hearing this and said that Ranvir never told her about Noor. On the other side, Harry asked Ranvir if they could go on a double date someday. While Ranvir hesitated to say anything, Noor immediately said yes.

After Ibaadat and Harry left the place, Ranvir questioned Noor, "Who do you think you are and what were you doing in front of them?"

"Relax, Ranvir, didn't you see Ibaadat's face when I said that I am your girlfriend. Dude, what is the problem with you?"

"Hold on, miss, you are going too fast. I don't want to start anything with anyone. But the drama which you started a few minutes ago needs to be finished, which is only possible if you continue to be my fake girlfriend in front of Ibaadat."

"You don't worry about that Ranvir. We will be a great couple." Noor winked and smiled. Noor was determined to bring Ranvir to the right track of life. At that point, Noor was utterly unaware of who Ranvir was. But still, she decided to help him out.

Ranvir decided to drop Noor at her place. The drive was filled with a deadly silence with a bit of conversation. However, the stereo was playing sad songs from the 2000s. Noor thought of asking Ranvir to change the channel, but she didn't say it.

They reached Noor's place in half an hour. Noor broke the deadly silence by saying goodbye.

Ranvir replied the same with a smile. But before getting out of the car, she said something to Ranvir which didn't let him sleep that night.

87

Chapter 12

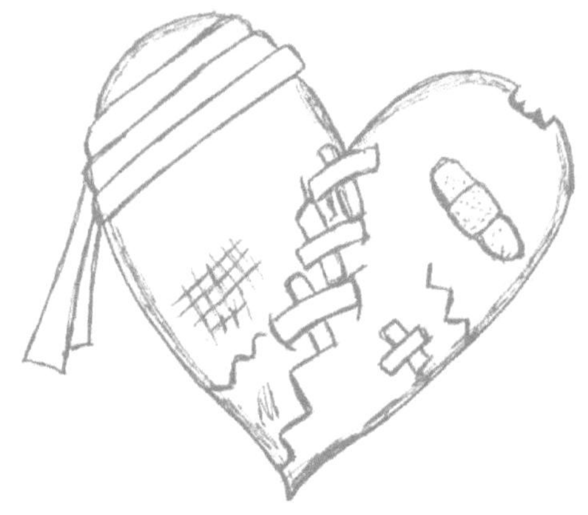

After dropping Noor , Ranvir came back home. As he entered the house, his mom told him that I was sitting on the roof. He came directly to me with two beer bottles.

"So, my boy, how was your first date with Noor? Can I expect that something great will happen between you two? Did you talk to her about

Ravneet?" I threw a mountain of questions at him.

"Hold on, Sahil. Who do you think I am? It was just a regular talk over a cup of coffee." Ranvir replied.

"Are you sure? Your face is telling me a different story. No problem buddy, now you will keep things secret, huh?"

"I was just kidding, Sahil. Let me tell you what happened there. When I got there, she was already waiting for me. We talked for a while but I saw Ibaadat entering the restaurant with Harry."

"Fuck man, did she ruin your date?"

"No, buddy, I did that to her this time. Actually, Noor did that."

I was delighted to hear that. I believed that Noor was the right girl to bring Ranvir on the right track. "Oh, so that is the reason for your smile."

"And you know what? Noor told Ibaadat that we had been dating each other for three years. Ibaadat went into shock after hearing that. Also, Harry wanted to go on a double date with us."

When Ranvir said that, I was also shocked. "What! Noor said that to Ibaadat." Ranvir replied with a yes. After which, I started laughing out loud. He tried to stop me, but I couldn't resist.

"But there is something more, which I believe you must know. When I dropped Noor home, she said something that made me think during the entire drive home."

Ranvir quoted Noor, "You don't have to forgive or take revenge when you have to move on. You can move on without any of those things happening. You just become different, and then you move on."

After saying this, Ranvir asked me what should be done. I thought on the same for some time, and then I replied to him in a sarcastic tone.

"Bro, don't ask me for relationship advice. The first one I give is to never get into a relationship. And the second one, my favourite, is break-up."

"Hey, that's not fair, bro. You are the one who set me up with her. And now, it is your responsibility to give me advice on the same."

I started laughing after hearing that and said that he should not take advice from me. Meanwhile, Ranvir's phone started buzzing. The phone showed text messages from Ibaadat.

Ibaadat- Hi Ranvir, how are you?

Ibaadat- Harry was asking to go on a double date. I don't think it is a good idea. What do you think?

Ranvir thought for some time and then replied.

Ranvir- I believe that we should go on one. At least we four will get a chance to get to know each other.

Ibaadat- Okay. If you think so, then it is alright. I will let Harry know.

Ranvir- Sure.

Ibaadat- Bbye, Take care.

Ranvir- Yeah, you too.

"So now you are going on a double date, huh. Just call Noor and tell her about that." I asked Ranvir to call Noor immediately. Noor's number was busy, so Ranvir said that he would call her later.

After having dinner at Ranvir's place, I went home. Later that night, Ranvir called Noor again. She picked up the phone and told him to text her instead of a call.

Ranvir- Hi, Ibaadat asked me for the double date again.

Noor- Okay!

Ranvir- I called you earlier to inform you, but you didn't pick up the call. I think you are still busy so we will talk about this later.

Before Noor could see the message, Ranvir said goodbye without having a proper conversation which could be pretty annoying. After some time, Noor texted him back.

Noor- Sorry, I was a little busy with my work. Did you say yes?

Ranvir- Of course. You were the one who initiated that. I just texted to inform you that we will be going on a date soon.

Noor- When?

Ranvir- I don't know. Harry is planning all of this.

Noor- Okay, just confirm it from Harry and let me know.

Ranvir- Thank you so much.

Noor- No problem, buddy. I called you my friend once, and now there is no stepping back.

Ranvir- Thanks again. I hope you know that I am doing all this just for Ibaadat.

Noor- Yes, completely. Don't worry. I have understood what kind of guy you are.

Ranvir- You think so? Good for you.

Noor- Don't worry Mr. Ranvir, I will be there. Bbye.

Ranvir- Bbye, Take care.

Noor- Yeah, you too.

Ranvir realised that Noor said bye in the same manner as he said to Ibaadat. So, he sensed what Noor might be feeling after he said that he was doing all this for Ibaadat.

Somewhere, in the back of his heart, Ranvir had a little spark of feelings for Noor, but he was afraid that it would burn his heart again.

Chapter 13

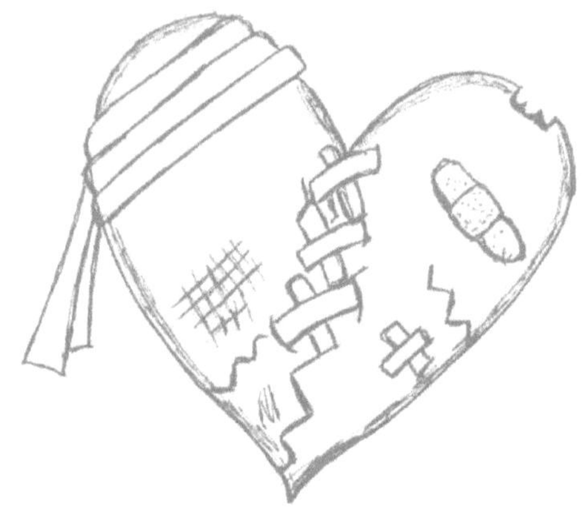

anvir was getting ready for the double date while I was helping him pick up the clothes to wear. "Are you sure that you want to do this?" I questioned him about what he was going to do in the next few hours

I knew that it would have devastating effects on him as well as on Noor. Going on a double date was never a good idea, but Ranvir thought he could get something out of it. But, he was unaware that he would lose much more than gain.

He took his car and went to pick up Noor. The time was 6 o' clock in the evening. Ranvir called Noor after reaching her place. Noor asked him to wait for 5 minutes which annoyed Ranvir as he was on time.

But after 5 minutes, he saw Noor coming out of her house, wearing a royal blue dress. She was looking incredibly pretty, so 5 minutes were worth waiting for.

"I don't like waiting, but I can do that for her." Ranvir thought in his mind while she entered the car. Ranvir told Noor that she was looking gorgeous in that dress.

In the meanwhile, Ibaadat shared the restaurant's location. Ranvir saw the message and started smiling. Noor asked for the reason behind the smile, but then she saw Ibaadat's chat opened in Ranvir's phone. She said nothing and kept quiet throughout their way to the restaurant.

Ranvir tried to have a conversation, but Noor was not in the mood to talk. Finally, after 30 minutes of driving, they reached the place as told by Ibaadat. Ranvir escorted Noor outside the car and requested her to act as planned.

It was a rooftop restaurant with a beautiful city view and sunset view on the other side. It was one of the finest restaurants in Amritsar, with half of sitting covered under glass and half of sitting in the open. Noor was sure that Harry would brag about the restaurant as it was tough to get a reservation in such a short time.

When they entered the restaurant, they saw Ibaadat and Harry sitting at a table. Noor put her hands on Ranvir's arms to make it look natural. Then, they greeted each other and sat in their respective seats.

It was cold that evening, and Ibaadat used to get affected by the common cold promptly. So, she asked Harry to get the tables shifted. Harry taunted, "Ibaadat, do you even know how much it cost to get a reservation here? I don't think that they will allow us to sit inside the glass."

Ranvir smiled and questioned, "Can you at least try asking?" Harry went to the manager and asked him if he could do something. The manager immediately said no to that, which was very embarrassing for Harry."

Harry came back and said that he couldn't get a table inside. Ranvir again smiled, and this time it was in a taunting way. Seeing that, Harry got frustrated and asked Ranvir if he could do something.

Ranvir called one of the attendants and asked him to call the manager. Within a minute, the manager was there. Ranvir asked him to get the sitting arrangements done in the VIP corner, which was the best point for the city view. After 5 minutes, they were sitting inside a glass room.

Ibaadat, in a low voice, asked Ranvir if he knew the manager, to which Ranvir replied, "Yes, he works for me. Actually, I am the owner of this restaurant." This was shocking for everyone listening to him. Noor looked at him with annoyance, but she kept calm.

Harry was more embarrassed after hearing that and started looking into the menu. Ibaadat thought that not only her but Ranvir also kept so many things to himself.

Ranvir insisted Noor and Ibaadat to place the order. Looking into the menu, Noor thought that Ranvir could have told at least her about the restaurant.

Ranvir asked Harry, "So what do you do for a living?" Harry replied that he owned a truck back in Canada and had planned to get one more after going back. Ranvir looked at Ibaadat and smiled in a taunting way.

After having dinner, Noor and Ibaadat went to the restroom while Ranvir and Harry were sitting at the table. Ibaadat asked Noor, "Ranvir never talked about you. There was a time when Ranvir shared every single event of his life with me, but now he has so many secrets that sometimes I think I know nothing about him."

"Yeah, I felt the same way today."

"What? Didn't you know about the restaurant thing before?"

"No, Ranvir never told me about the restaurant."

"That's strange."

They went back to the table where Ranvir and Harry were sitting quietly. After a few minutes, Harry's phone started ringing, and he went to a side to attend the call.

Noor and Ibaadat continued the conversation, but this time it was loud enough for Ranvir to hear.

"Noor, you said that Ranvir never told you about the restaurant, right?" Ibaadat questioned, to which Noor Replied that she wasn't aware. Ibaadat turned her face towards Ranvir with disappointment.

"Ranvir, you were never like this. What happened to you?" Ibaadat questioned.

"There was a girl, who was my life, but she left me for a silly reason. She was the last person who knew everything about me. But now, I just don't tell anybody who I am. I just let them wonder who I am." Ranvir replied, staring into her eyes.

Ibaadat broke eye contact by turning her face down and said, "There was a boy, who was my everything. I used to believe that we were made for each other. He was the brightest star in the sky, but I lost him to the lights of the city of my dreams."

Noor tried to sneak out of the conversation by saying that she wanted another round of drinks. So now there were only two people on the table and just awkward silence. Ranvir broke the ice and said, "So this is what you needed in life, huh?"

"Sometimes, things don't work as we want them to. Sometimes, you have to leave things behind to start a new life. Just tell me how long can anyone hold the memories and live with them."

"I did, and I am still doing that. Why is it that you never noticed that I never moved on? I am still standing at the same place where you left me."

"Oh really? What about Noor? She said that you two have been dating for 3 long years."

"That's crap. We just met a few days back. I was just mad at you, and one day at the bar, I was drunk when I told Noor the entire story."

Ibaadat was shocked when Ranvir told her this. It was still unbelievable for her, but she seemed to like what Ranvir said then. By that time, Noor came back to the table with her drink.

"So, lovebirds, how are you doing?"

"Noor, do you mind if I ask you something?" Ibaadat said to Noor, to which she replied," Anything." Noor wasn't aware that Ranvir had told everything to Ibaadat, but she was pretty confident that she could answer anything.

"Are you his girlfriend, or are you just seeing each other?"

Noor was drunk, and she replied, "You tell me Ibaadat, If I throw you down from this building will you be dead, or will you just stop breathing?"

Ranvir started laughing out loud after hearing that. His laughter was loud enough to draw Harry's attention. Harry cut the call and came back to the table. He was in a hurry and said that he needed to go somewhere immediately. Ranvir said that he would drop Ibaadat home if Harry was Okay with that.

Harry was so busy with his call that he didn't bother. Instead, he said, "That would be great. Actually, I was going to book a cab for her. Thanks to you, man." Harry left the restaurant after saying that.

Chapter 14

After spending some time in the restaurant, they came outside. Noor tried to put her hand around Ranvir's arm, but Ranvir resisted. He explained to Noor, "I told Ibaadat that we met a few weeks ago. So, it's alright, you don't have to pretend to be my girlfriend anymore."

Noor got furious after hearing that. She said, "I was never here for this reason, and this is not why I wanted to hold your hand. But people like you have a problem of going back to the same person who tries to hurt you every time." She wanted to leave immediately, but Ranvir insisted that he would drop her home.

Ibaadat was listening to this, but she preferred to stay quiet. After this drama, they all got in the car. Ibaadat sat beside Ranvir while Noor sat in the back seat, cursing herself for accompanying Ranvir that day.

There was dead silence in the car till Ranvir dropped Noor at her place. Noor said goodbye to both of them; disappointed, she went inside the house. Ranvir put on the gear and started driving towards Ibaadat's home.

Dead silence continued till Ibaadat broke the ice. "Noor is a nice girl; you shouldn't have talked to her in that tone. Even if you met her a few weeks back, this is not the way to behave, Ranvir."

"Well, she wasn't you that I should have talked to her politely. You know there was a time I was nice to everyone, so kind and so sweet, but now I am like fuck this, fuck that and fuck everything."

"What is this Ranvir?" Ibaadat questioned.

"You want to know what this is, huh? This is what I have become after you left. All good inside me died the day you left, and the bad left behind got stronger when I got to know about Harry."

"What is the matter with you? You know this is the only reason that I never wanted you to know about Harry. I knew that you would never understand and would go mad."

"We were never going to work. But I wanted us to be you-me-we. It seems like a beautiful dream to me. The dream which you were afraid of getting true, and I was praying every day for it. But now it hardly matters, because you are with someone else." Ranvir said this and turned his face towards the road.

"Even I wanted us to be together, but with the Ranvir I knew, not the Ranvir that you have become," Ibaadat confronted Ranvir.

"We were in a relationship when kids of our age used to watch cartoons. You just cannot let anyone come and go from your life who has been this close to you. So, in order to heal, I took the path which didn't allow anyone else to go along with me."

Ranvir continued, "When you came back, I thought that I could live my life again. But I was wrong. You didn't even bother to think about me even when you were back."

"I didn't want to hurt you again and again, but eventually, I did," Ibaadat said in a low tone, after which Ranvir could see tears in her eyes.

"I didn't want to love you again and again, but eventually, I did too, and I am so sorry for that," Ranvir said this, and then there was complete silence for some time. Finally, Ibaadat said, "Sorry for everything Ranvir." To which Ranvir replied, "Thank you for everything. You made me the man I am today."

Both of them were on the verge of crying. Ranvir turned on the Radio to reduce the amount of tension. But the first song on the playlist was "We don't talk anymore."

Ranvir stopped the car on the side of the road and went outside. He was crying out loud. Ibaadat got out and went near him. Ranvir said, "You don't know about actual loss because that only occurs when you love something more than yourself. Don't you dare to love somebody that much."

"I love you. I am totally in love with you, and I don't care if it is too late; I am letting you know anyway." Ibaadat said and started crying. Ranvir faced her and said, "You should know if you come any closer; I am not letting you go."

Ranvir pulled her closer; Ibaadat didn't resist. Both their eyes were filled with tears. Ranvir held her tightly. Ibaadat's hands were over Ranvir's shoulders. They hugged each other. And in a few minutes, they were kissing each other.

Finally, Ibaadat got into her senses and realised that they were standing on the side of the lonely road and were getting late for home. So, she tried to tell Ranvir that they needed to leave that place, but Ranvir behaved like a little kid who didn't want Ibaadat to part from him.

"I love you so much Ibaadat. Please don't go away from me."

"I love you too Ranvir, more than anything else in this world, but you have to let me go. You have to let me let you go. I need you to do that for me."

And now, there was an awkward silence. It seemed like time had stopped. There was no sign of any human soul in their vicinity. Ranvir didn't want to make things worse, so he told Ibaadat, "We must get in the car and get going."

After that, they didn't talk to each other till they reached Ibaadat's place. Then, before Ibaadat got out of the car, she said, "I forgot to tell you that my engagement date has been fixed. It's next Sunday. I hope that you will be there."

Ranvir smiled in grief, and the pain behind his smile was pretty visible. Ibaadat continued, "Please, bring Noor along with you. I will take that as my engagement gift."

After saying this, she got out and went inside her house. Ranvir drove the car back to his place, and straightway went to his room. He didn't talk to anyone that night. He was severely in need of speaking to someone and some rest, but neither did he talk to anyone nor did he sleep that night.

Chapter 15

anvir had a very severe guilt trip for two reasons. The first one was that he cried in front of Ibaadat last night and the second one was that he misbehaved with Noor.

He came to my place to tell me everything that happened last night. The only thing that surprised and bothered me at the same time was that Ranvir and Ibaadat kissed each other. And that too when Ibaadat was about to get engaged.

I advised him to talk to Noor first and say sorry to her. So Ranvir called Noor and said sorry for last night. Noor was a little upset, but she accepted Ranvir's apology on one condition that they would go on a long drive and spend one day together.

Ranvir agreed to her condition, and they planned to go two days before Ibaadat's engagement. On one the side, Ranvir was worried about Ibaadat's engagement, while Noor was excited to spend a day together.

The day started at 6 in the morning, and they headed towards Chandigarh. Noor was completely in a picnic mood. As Ranvir began driving, she started talking and didn't stop till they came back. At first, Ranvir was annoyed, but later on, he started enjoying talking to her.

Noor said that she was a very reserved person, and Ranvir was one of the few people with whom she talked this much. Noor wanted to know Ranvir better, so she said that the conversation should not stop till the end of the day.

"So, what do you want to talk about?" Ranvir asked. Noor, after which she said, "I want to talk about you. Your hopes, your dreams and everything you want in life." Ranvir wanted to pretend cool, so he said, "Just to be clear, I am too smart to be seduced by these words."

Noor liked that confidence level instilled in Ranvir, even after a tragic love story. And probably this was the only thing she adored about Ranvir. He was honest with her, even if he was rude, but he didn't lie to her at any point in time.

"Have you ever felt yourself not welcome somewhere, not invited?" Noor asked Ranvir. Ranvir thought who could probably know him better than a girl in front of whom he had surrendered himself and his story when he was drunk at the bar.

But he replied, "Nah, I feel like people are waiting for me in a queue." Noor knew that it was sarcastic, and she was expecting it to be. "I believe that you don't trust people easily. Can you tell me why?"

"You say that I should trust people? I don't feel like trusting anyone because the one person I thought would never turn on me turned on me. The one person I thought would never hurt me, hurt me. The one person I thought would never leave me, left me. So, tell me why?" Ranvir's eyes were filled with tears.

"Because there are still some people out there who won't turn back on you, hurt you or leave you," Noor replied, grabbing his hand. She wanted to assure him that she was the one who could fix him.

But Ranvir was in a different mode, "I don't need you to fix me. I need you to take care of me while I fix myself. But love is something that is gone from my life. I cannot handle that stuff anymore."

The awkward silence was pervasive when Ranvir was with any girl. Noor was, however, determined to talk to Ranvir, so she again continued, "You know Ranvir, I am just a normal human being. If anything funny happens around me, I laugh, and if anything miserable happens, I cry. And you know it is much better than pretending that you are strong while you are a weak little boy."

"You call me weak? Huh, I have seen a person going from loving me every day to acting like I never existed. When you dare to see that, then come and talk to me." Ranvir replied in an angry tone.

"Ha-ha, do you think that by saying this, you will become strong?"

"Don't put me in a position where I have to show you how heartless I can be. You might never look at me in the same way." Ranvir said this, and after that, there was no conversation for a few hours.

Noor was furious at Ranvir again, Ranvir felt guilty again, and there was an awkward silence in the car again. Ranvir stopped the car at a highway plaza and got some ice cream for Noor.

Noor cooled down after having ice cream, and Ranvir promised that he wouldn't fight with her till the trip was over. Noor said, "Look at me Ranvir, I reject at least 10 proposals every day. But your vibes hit differently when we first met. Just because of your innocence, I fell for you. And you, on the other hand, still want to go after the girl who has a habit of breaking your heart again and again."

"You know Noor, some things are unexplainable. You don't choose who you love. You just fall in love with the person. It's never about outer beauty. I believe that souls are connected. And I am so connected to Ibaadat that even if I am on my deathbed and she tells me to get up, I swear I will defeat death and get up for her." Ranvir explained his love for Ibaadat.

"Wow Ranvir, I wish that someday, someone will love me the way you love Ibaadat," Noor replied. They spent the rest of the day together in Chandigarh and came back. Noor's affection for Ranvir grew heartier.

Before getting out of the car, Noor said, "I love you, Ranvir, and I want you to know that. But today I didn't come here to tell you this. It's not that I cannot live without you. I can live, but the thing is, I don't want to."

But Ranvir said, "Okay, good night then. I will pick you up the day after tomorrow at 10."

"Seriously? Is this the way you reply to a girl when she says that she loves you?"

"Noor, we have already talked about this the entire time. But I promise you one thing. If I ever fell in love again, you will be the first one to know." Ranvir said, looking into her eyes. Noor blushed after hearing this and said good night to Ranvir.

Ranvir called me and said, "Bro, isn't it amazing? That one person kills my heart while the other one is trying to make it better. And look at me, foolish enough, unable to make a choice."

I said, "What happened to you, bro? Who got you thinking like that? Don't say that you are in love again."

"No bro, Noor is a nice girl, but I am not in love with her. But the way she cares about me and that's what made me think about her. You know, after my break-up, I vowed to never fall in love again. But, now, when I think about her, my heart whispers, one more time, please."

"This is what people call healing. Just take care of yourself and drive back safe, we will meet the day after tomorrow." After that, I hung up the phone and felt that finally, there could be some peace in Ranvir's life.

After a few seconds, I received a text message from Ranvir.

Ranvir- Bro, I forgot to tell you that Noor said I love you to me, but I said OKAY, Good Night. And now, I regret that. That message made me think that Ranvir was a complete idiot.

The peace which I was expecting in his life seemed very far for him. I wanted to make everything right but things were way out of my control.

Chapter 16

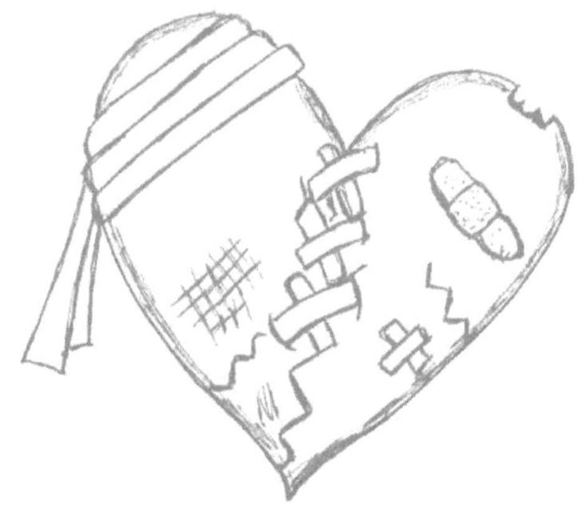

anvir was standing in front of the mirror, getting ready for Ibaadat's ring ceremony. But, he felt as if he was about to lose the most important person in his life.

Suited-booted and disheartened, Ranvir went to pick up Noor at her place. She was already waiting for him, dressed up in a blue outfit. Noor was aware that it was an excruciating moment in Ranvir's life, and she wanted to make him feel as happy as she could.

I was waiting for him at the venue. Ibaadat's parents spent a lot of money on that party, and it was quite evident. Harry stood with his friends, waiting for the arrival of Ibaadat.

Ibaadat called Ranvir to check whether he was coming or not. But Ranvir didn't pick up the phone as he was with Noor. So Ibaadat called me to inquire, and I confirmed that Ranvir had gone to Noor's place.

When Ranvir arrived at the party hall, I texted Ibaadat about his arrival. After 5 minutes, she came out. She wore an ethnic lehenga, looking extremely beautiful. All eyes were on Ibaadat, but her eyes were searching for only one person at that time.

When Ibaadat and Ranvir saw each other, there was a halt in time. They recalled all the moments they spent together, Ranvir's face was miserable since morning, but he tried to smile in front of

Ibaadat. She smiled back and turned her face towards Harry.

A few moments later, they were ready to exchange rings. Harry was looking at Ibaadat, wondering about his destiny, but Ibaadat was looking everywhere else. Finally, they exchanged the rings, and Ranvir's love shattered into dust.

Noor held Ranvir's hand tightly and said, "Don't worry buddy, some things are just out of control. If you stop loving her, you will suffer for a short time, but if you continue to stay like this, the pain will never stop, and one day you will be dead with this pain."

Ranvir said that it was not the right time to talk and went to the bar. He got a large whiskey for himself. Noor followed him and sat near Ranvir with her glass of wine. Within no time, Ranvir gulped five large whiskeys.

He was still sober and asked for more. Noor tried to stop him, but he wasn't listening to anyone. Finally, Noor was frustrated and said, "Seriously? Ranvir, now this is getting out of control, and you need to stop right now."

Ranvir replied, "You don't know about the actual loss until and unless you love someone so deep and that person leaves you in this way. So, when you feel that, come to me, then we will talk."

Noor got fuming hot and said, "Ranvir, dating is supposed to be fun, a relationship is supposed to be fun, seeing each other is supposed to be fun, and even love is supposed to be fun, but people like you have a mentality that you have to suffer first to deserve something decent. And you know what? Your expectation of decent is not even decent after you get it."

Ranvir smiled at Noor and suddenly said out loud, "Thank you so much. Now get the fuck out of here." He broke the glass in his hand.

Noor held Ranvir's hand and took him to Ibaadat, standing with Harry in the centre of the hall. Then, she went close to her and said, "Do you love Ranvir?"

Everyone standing there was shocked. At first, Ibaadat looked like what the hell is this girl saying, but then she said yes and turned her face towards Ranvir. Ranvir was stunned after hearing that.

Noor continued, "Were you ever going to tell Ranvir about this?"

"No," Ibaadat replied.

Noor questioned Ranvir, "Did that hurt?"

Ranvir made a weird face and didn't reply to Noor. Noor patted his shoulder and said, "Welcome to the last 20 days of my life." After saying that, she just started walking outside, leaving Ranvir and Ibaadat confused.

After walking a few steps, Noor came back to Ibaadat and said, "Since you are good at reading people's minds, I am pretty sure that you won't have any trouble in reading this one." Then, Noor showed her middle finger to Ibaadat and went away.

Harry didn't want any drama to start between Ibaadat and Ranvir, so he yelled at Ranvir, "Get the fuck out of here." However, Ranvir kept his calm, looked at Ibaadat, smiled and went outside.

I wanted to escort him out, but something was pending to be done inside the party hall. So, I went to Ibaadat and said, "He trusted you blindly and walked wherever you wanted, and all you did was just hold his hand and get him off the track. He fell in love with what he saw and what he heard, and every time all you did was just lie to him."

I always wanted to say this to Ibaadat but was waiting for a perfect moment, and it couldn't have been better than this. After saying that, I went after Ranvir to keep a check upon him.

Ranvir was standing in the parking lot. He leaned his back on the car and was staring at the sky. When I approached him, he started smiling. Then, he hugged me tightly, and I said, "Ranvir, please do me a favour. Cry for some time, and I want you to do that in front of me."

He started crying out loud, and I didn't stop him from doing that. I just told him that no one would come back for him and we should get going. So, I drove him back home. While we were heading back, he said, "I told Ibaadat what hurt me the most, and she did every bit of that perfectly. You know buddy, today I saw a stranger in those eyes in which once I saw my soulmate."

I stayed at Ranvir's place that night and watched that poor soul cribbing for a girl. Before going off to sleep, he was saying one line continuously, "I once loved her so much that I tried to fix her while she was breaking me."

There were only three days left for Ibaadat's departure from this city and Ranvir's life. So, I literally prayed that night for everything to go smoothly. I stayed with Ranvir for the entire three days.

Chapter 17

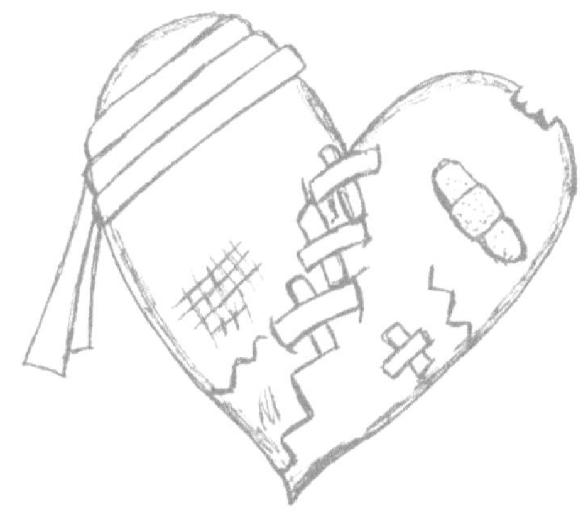

e were sitting on the roof, talking about Ranvir's life when he said, "You know, sometimes when I am alone at night, I really don't know how I feel. I am not really sad and not so happy either. I don't know what is happening around me. I can see that; I can feel that as well, but I don't know what should I do about it."

There are some moments in life when all the odds are against you. Of course, you want everything to be correct. But things are way out of your control. Ranvir was going through that phase in life. I didn't want to give him any moral lecture at that time so, I just thought of settling things up with a bottle of Teachers.

As he opened the bottle, he recalled his first meeting with Noor. He smiled for a while and said that Noor would never forgive him. Then, after four pegs, he closed his hand and showed them to me.

"Buddy, in my left hand, there are memories of Ibaadat and me together, and in my right hand, I see Noor eagerly waiting for me. If I choose left, then there is nothing right, and if I go for right, there is nothing left."

I felt pity for Ranvir and said, "It's your life bro, you cannot live with someone's memories. And before loving anyone else, just love yourself." He kept quiet after that, and we just sat there for another two hours.

The clock was ticking at 12 when we both were 1 bottle down. Ranvir asked me to drive to

Ibaadat's house. "Are you crazy, bro? At this time, in this condition, and that too when she would be gone from your life the day after tomorrow?" The bottle I had drunk went for a six. And suddenly, I was sober again in all senses.

"You have just gone out of control, brother. I cannot take you there right now." I said.

"Look, if you don't drive me there, then I will go by myself. Now that's what you want, huh?" Ranvir replied and went inside the room to search for the car keys. I went chasing him down.

"Did you forget that I drove the car back home?" I took out the keys and told him to wear good clothes if he wanted to go out. As we reached there, I warned him that it was neither the right time nor the right place to talk to Ibaadat. But he didn't stop and rang the doorbell.

Ibaadat's mom opened the door. Ranvir asked her to send Ibaadat outside. His face was red hot in anger, and Ibaadat's mom sensed that. She said that Ibaadat had gone out with her friends. Ranvir got mad and started shouting out her name loudly.

Unfortunately, Ibaadat was at home and listened to Ranvir yelling her name. She came outside, and Ranvir started shouting, "I should have known that your love was just a game, but it was damn true from my side. Fucking, I can't get you out of my heart. Why don't you just go away?"

"What are you saying, Ranvir? Why are you saying all this?" Ibaadat was shocked

"I hate you, don't show me your face ever," he said.

"Are you going to be like this? Then I hate you too," she started crying.

"Why do you hate me? I have been chasing you for six fucking years. I didn't cheat on you. I have prayed for you with every single breath. But you proved yourself unworthy of my love. And now I don't fucking care whatever you do." He said that loud and clear.

It was totally unbelievable to my eyes what Ranvir did that night. Ibaadat was standing right in front of him crying, and he started walking away from her. At that time, even I was worried about Ibaadat. "Try to save your hate against me for the upcoming days. There is a lot more which you have to see before you leave this country." These were his final words to her.

He came back to the car and told me to drive back home. The car barely moved away from her house, and he started crying, loud enough to make me stop the car. He was slapping himself, trying to punish himself for what he had done a few moments ago.

I was worried, much more for Ibaadat than for Ranvir. He was sitting right next to me, punishing himself while Ibaadat was still standing at the gate, wondering about what had happened to her in the last few minutes.

Love is the most beautiful and most potent double-edged weapon; you will be attracted to it, try to bring it close to yourself, try to feel it, and you won't realise that it is destroying you until and unless it makes you bleed. But it was too late for Ranvir and Ibaadat to learn the same.

Somehow, I took Ranvir back home. Ranvir denied sleeping that night, and due to this reason, I too remained awake. Finally, he fell asleep at 5 in the morning.

A day before her departure Ibaadat texted Ranvir.

Ibaadat- still angry?

Ranvir- I am sorry for yesterday. I don't know why I did that. I was drunk.

Ibaadat- I am sorry for ruining everything again.

Ranvir- I had no idea that Noor would say all that. But your answer to her question was yes.

Ibaadat- Because I was afraid.

Ranvir- Afraid of what?

Ibaadat- Losing my best friend.

Ranvir- Hey, don't say that now. You know what? Everything I was afraid of happening just happened.

Ibaadat- There is something that you need to know. For that, I want you to come to the airport tomorrow before I depart.

Ranvir- Ibaadat, I am sick and tired of this thing.

Ibaadat- Please, just for us.

Ranvir- I have realised that we are born alone, and we will die alone. It's just a bunch of people that come and go. And I am living like there is no tomorrow.

Ibaadat- Why are you saying that?

Ranvir- Because there isn't one without you.

Ibaadat tried calling Ranvir after that, but he didn't pick the phone. Although he decided to go and see Ibaadat once at the airport, he didn't tell Ibaadat about this.

The following day, we went to the airport. Ibaadat was already there, standing with her family. Ranvir bought a bouquet for her at the airport. He was standing still and didn't even take a single step towards Ibaadat.

Finally, after saying a final goodbye to the family, Ibaadat came near Ranvir. Ranvir gave the bouquet to her, and they said final adieu to each other. Ibaadat said, "I miss the person you were." And started walking away from him.

Epilogue

anvir completely forgot the reason for which he came to the airport that day. He didn't ask Ibaadat about what she was going to say. He texted Ibaadat regarding the same but got no reply as she got busy with check-in formalities.

I inquired if Ibaadat replied to Ranvir. He handed over his phone to me to see the inbox. Then, Ranvir told me to take the cab back home and started running towards the parking lot.

"Hey bro, where are you going?" I questioned.

"I think I need to sort out things with Noor. I believe that she is waiting for me." He straight away took the car and went to Noor's place, leaving his phone behind with me.

After reaching there, he got to know that she wasn't there. Then he recalled that he had left his phone with me. So, he took someone's phone and called me to take Noor's number.

After getting Noor's number, Ranvir called her. But, she didn't pick the phone the first time, Ranvir tried again, but she didn't answer. Finally, she responded to his call.

Ranvir- Oh, thank God! Hello love

Noor- Who is this?

Ranvir- Has it been that long?

Noor- Ranvir, is that you?

Ranvir- Yes, sweetheart, it's me. Where are you right now?

Noor- Just entered the clinic. What happened?

Ranvir- A lot. I am coming to you in the next 30 mins.

Noor- Hey, drive safe, stupid.

Noor was waiting outside for Ranvir. As he arrived, the first thing Noor asked was, "Did she break your heart again?"

"Yes, but this time it was just a scratch," Ranvir replied and passed an embarrassing smile. After which, Noor said, "Good, you deserved some of those. So why are you here?"

Ranvir explained, "People who need love the most ask for it in the most unloving way. It sounds crazy, but somehow they are seeking love. And I came here seeking love, the love which I believe I can get from you. I love you, Noor."

"I'll take you back even when you don't say sorry. It doesn't mean that I am weak. It just means that I feel too strongly for you. I love you too, Ranvir." Noor smiled and hugged him tightly.

Ranvir continued, "I love everything about you, and I am not a guy who says that lightly; I am a guy who has searched for love my entire life in the wrong person. I thought love was just something that idiots thought they felt. But you got a hold on my heart that I could not break even if I wanted to."

After everything was over, I reached there by cab, frustrated but, when I saw Ranvir and Noor, all the frustration went for six. Noor took the day off from work, and we celebrated that day.

We reached home late in the evening, and we were sitting on the roof. Ranvir asked me if Ibaadat texted back. I said no to that question and told him to just forget about her. After which, he said, "I have realised that the only person I ever lost in my life and needed back was me. I was moving towards hell. But Noor taught me to live."

Ranvir decided to get married, and Noor was ready for that too. So next year, they got married, and within three years, I became an uncle to Ranvir's son.

Something was galloping inside me, which I needed to tell someone from the last four years. So, I chose Noor to say the same. While Ranvir was away at work, I went to Noor and showed her the messages Ibaadat sent before departing.

Ibaadat- The only thing I wanted you to know was that on the day of my engagement, I came outside for you, leaving everything behind.

Ibaadat- Also, Harry broke up with me that day, but I didn't care.

Ibaadat- I have always loved you Ranvir and will continue to love you forever. So even if you call me after reading my messages, I am ready to come back.

Noor was shocked after reading that thread of messages. I smiled and said, "I told Ranvir that Ibaadat never texted him back and deleted all the messages from his phone after copying them in mine. She was tu rning the pages every fucking time, so I burnt the whole book in the end."

Noor said, "You are evil, but thank you so much. We are finally living a good life together, and the enormous credit goes to you."

"Don't underestimate the power of evil buddy, even the purest of hearts are attracted to it," I winked and smiled.

"There was a time when we loved watching superheroes fighting evil. But now we understand the villain and his intentions and circumstances behind being evil too." I explained the reason behind my actions.

"By the way, Ravneet is a nice girl to date. Can you set me up with her?" I asked Noor, and she gave me a teasing look.

We both went into flashbacks and were lost in the space of time. Then, Noor started thinking about Ibaadat and said that although much time has passed, Ranvir still remembers his wonderful time together with Ibaadat.

"That's why he keeps on saying this after drinking, 'I know that I have to stop loving her. But can I take a little more time, maybe forever?'...Oops, I believe that I shouldn't have told you this," I said, and we kept on laughing at that for hours.

THE END

About the Author

Doubty Noble is an officer in the Indian Army and is an author of "When you fall in love and war." He loves to write heartwarming stories with a somewhat happy ending and a lot of mess happening along the way. He wants to leave a mark in people's heart through his writings and want people to derive sweet but painful lessons from his stories.

He has met many people around in his career, and everyone had a different story. So he got inspired by their stories and decided to frame them in his words. He believes that when people tell their stories, they heal their hearts. When he is not writing, he loves to sketch, play volleyball and spend time with his close ones untangling their lives.

Printed by Libri Plureos GmbH in Hamburg, Germany